MISTLETOE MAGIC

A COLLECTION OF CHRISTMAS ROMANCES

JENNY MARIE TAYLOR   PATRICIA WILSON

ANNE LUCY-SHANLEY   AMBER TERRELL

AMANDA JEMMETT   NIKOLETT STRACHAN

MISTLETOE MAGIC: A COLLECTION OF CHRISTMAS ROMANCES
Copyright © 2021 ANNE LUCY-SHANLEY, JENNY MARIE TAYLOR,
PATRICIA WILSON, AMBER TERRELL, AMANDA JEMMETT, NIKOLETT
STRACHAN
EBOOK ISBN: 978-1-9991594-6-7
PRINT ISBN: 978-1-9991594-7-4
Cover art by Amanda Jemmett

❀ Created with Vellum

CONTENTS

A CHRISTMAS CORGI

BY JENNY MARIE TAYLOR

NOVEMBER 19

I AM A GOOD LISTENER.

I know this because my first owner, Miss Loretta, told me so every day. She was very old and didn't have many friends, so I would sit in her lap and listen to her tell stories of her life. Sometimes her stories were very long, and I wanted to play outside, but it made her so happy to pet my head and talk to me. So I listened.

Right after my first birthday, Miss Loretta got sick. She had to lay in bed all day. Strangers came in and out to take care of her. It was a scary time. I don't like to think about it.

Soon after that, Miss Loretta stopped telling stories, then she stopped talking at all. They took her away in a big bag, and I spent all day waiting at the door for her to come home.

But she didn't. Instead, a man named Rick showed up. I met him before. He seemed very nice and very quiet. He came with a new lady, Lillian. I was excited because she had a poofy scarf around her neck, and she smelled like flowers.

Lillian shooed me away when I jumped on her and sat at Miss Loretta's table full of papers. She shuffled through the papers for a long time, while Rick sat on the couch. He looked sad, so I gave him kisses while Lillian huffed and moved papers around.

"This is a complete mess, Rick. Didn't you ever check on your mother?"

"Of course I did. Mom was an accountant. I assumed she had taken care of these things."

"Ridiculous. This will take weeks to sort through." She glared at me while Rick patted my head. "And don't get attached to that mutt. I despise dogs almost as much as I despise children."

"This isn't a mutt, Lillian. It's a corgi. Mom loved this dog."

Lillian slammed her hands on the table, scaring Rick and me.

"Forget it! My head is pounding. I'm going to go lay down. This day has been exhausting for me."

I was grateful when Lillian went into the bedroom.

"Don't listen to her, little fella. I'm sure she'll come around in the morning."

Little lines of water trickled down Rick's face. He looked sad. I felt sad, too. I whined and kissed his hands and he patted my head until he fell asleep. I didn't leave his side. I was too scared of Lillian.

That day I learned that I can't trust people just because they smell like flowers.

NOVEMBER 20

THE NEXT MORNING, Lillian picked me up and put me in the car before Rick woke up. I was excited to go somewhere new, but a little scared of where Lillian would take me. She didn't seem to like me, no matter how many kisses I tried to give her. We drove for a long time before Lillian said anything. "It's not your fault, you know. Loretta never should have gotten a dog at her age. She was never a practical woman. Talking to Rick you would think she was some kind of saint, but she had many flaws."

Lillian continued to say bad things about Loretta. I didn't want to be a good listener now. She was being very mean. I tried covering my ears with my paws, but I could still hear her. Finally, she pulled the car into a dirt road. I looked out the window and could see a small house with a barn behind it. There were no other houses close by. I could hear some dogs from behind the barn, and that got me excited.

"Come along, mutt," Lillian said and grabbed me hard. I wanted to bite her, but I didn't think Miss Loretta would've liked it if I did.

A man walked up to us. He had curly hair on his head and hair on his face. I never saw a man with hair on his face before, and it scared me. I growled and showed him my teeth so he wouldn't think about hurting me.

"Oh my goodness! What are you doing, sweetheart? I'm so sorry, Mr. Richland. He's normally such a docile animal."

"It's fine," the man said and took me from Lillian's arms. He looked scary, but he held me gently and scratched my throat in my favorite spot. "This is a girl, by the way. What's her name?"

Lillian stared at the man blankly. "Teacup," she finally answered. That was not what Miss Loretta called me. Miss Loretta always called me "Sweetie."

The man laughed. "That's a stupid name."

Lillian didn't like that. She said something under her breath and put her sunglasses back on. "Well, I'll be on my way."

"Wait! Don't you have any of her things? Where are her shot records? What kind of food does she eat?"

"I must have forgotten them. I'll bring them by this after-noon," Lillian said as she got in the car. She shut the door, smiled, and waved as she drove away.

"Shew, you dodged a bullet there," the man said, scratching my throat. "I'm Mike. Welcome to Wyatt Rescue. We're gonna find you a nice, new family. But first, let's get some breakfast."

I wagged my tail. I hadn't eaten for two whole days. Mike seemed like a nice man, even with his hairy face.

That day I learned you can trust a human even if they have hair on their face.

NOVEMBER 25

OVER THE NEXT FEW DAYS, I got used to the farm. Mike liked to talk to me the way Miss Loretta did. It made me miss her a little less. I followed Mike around while he helped the animals around the farm. I think he enjoyed my company as much as I enjoyed his. He even let me stay in his trailer at night. I was the only dog there who was allowed to do that.

"You know, I haven't been working here too long myself. You're the first rescue drop-off since I got here, Coco." That was what he called me. I liked my new name.

There was another person that worked on the farm, Celia. Mike seemed to like her very much. He didn't talk to her often, but he talked about her a lot.

One day she walked up to him after taking care of the horses. "Hey, Mike. I need a favor."

"Sure. Anything."

"Could my daughter, Amelia, come by after school and hang with you for a couple of hours a day? My boss told me she can't stay at the restaurant anymore, and her father is useless. She's a really good kid. She can help you with whatever you need. I promise she'll be no trouble at all. I can't afford to pay you much…"

"Of course! I love kids. And you don't have to pay me. I'm happy to help."

"Really? That's such a major help, you have no idea. My mom is working every day, and since Grammy had that stroke, Papa is so busy taking care of her I hate to ask him for help. I don't have anyone I can count on."

"Well, you've got me." Mike gave her a huge smile.

"Thanks so much. I'll call the school and let them know. I'll pick her up around six!"

Mike watched her until she was out of sight, then turned to me. "Isn't she cool?"

I didn't know what that meant, but from the look on Mike's face, it must have been a good thing.

"Everything about her is perfect. I even love the stuff about her that I can't stand. Like the fact that she blasts country music in here, or how she's always bossing me around and nagging me for eating junk food. Something is wrong with me."

That was the first day I met Amelia. She ran off of a big bus full of kids and came right to me.

"Is that a corgi?!"

Mike laughed. "Yeah. Her name is Coco. She's a great dog."

"Mommy didn't tell me you guys got a corgi!"

She was the smallest person I had ever seen. And she was missing a tooth in the front, so her s's whistled. Miss Loretta was missing a lot of teeth, but she didn't whistle.

Amelia had so much energy, we ran around for hours. I never had so much fun! I was sad when Celia took her away. I whined at the car while it was driving away, but Mike promised that I would see her again the next day.

That day I learned that little people with missing teeth are the most fun.

NOVEMBER 26

THIS WAS a scary day for me. Mike woke me up in the morning and told me that a group of people called a "family" were coming to look at me, and maybe take me home. I didn't know what he meant because I already was at home. Later that day, a car pulled up and a man and woman got out. They seemed nice enough, but then two humans even smaller than Amelia jumped out and ran right at me. They came at me so fast I didn't have a chance to run away. They looked exactly the same, and had the same clothes on. It was confusing. One of them pulled my ear and the other grabbed my tail. I whined and tried to get away, but the one that had my tail wouldn't let go.

The man laughed at me and said, "Boys! Let go of the doggy. She isn't ours yet!"

Mike rushed over and picked me up. I was thankful that he was there to protect me.

The man poked his hand at Mike and said, "I'm Jordan. We spoke on the phone. I'm here to pick up the corgi. I'm assuming this is the one?"

Mike frowned at the man, but he took his hand and shook it up and down. "I'm Mike. There's a little more to it than that. We need to make sure you're a good match."

"Oh hell, we're a perfect match!"

"Honey! Language," the woman yelled at Jordan. She held a tiny human, smaller than me. I didn't know people could get so small. I thought it was cute, but suddenly it let out a screeching sound worse than anything I had ever heard.

Jordan and Mike continued to talk, but I couldn't understand what they were saying over the piercing screeches of the tiny human.

Finally, the woman got back in the car. She was frowning and her voice sounded mean and upset. "Just hurry it up, Jordan. I'm going to nurse Clara in the car," she said as she slammed the car door shut.

"Right, enough chit chat. Do I need to sign anything?"

Mike held me higher as the double humans jumped up to grab at me.

"I'm sorry, Jordan, this isn't going to work."

Jordan dropped his smile. "Excuse me?"

"I don't think your family is ready for a dog. Maybe try a hamster or something."

Jordan got closer to Mike's face. I growled at him.

"Is that supposed to be funny? I drove two hours to get here. I'm getting this dog."

Mike took a step toward Jordan. He was so brave! "Not from this rescue you're not. This is my dog now. I suggest you leave this property."

Jordan said many mean words to Mike, and the small double humans started screaming. They eventually got back in their car, and I was never happier to see people leave.

Later that day, the small box that Mike carried with him everywhere started ringing, and he put it to his ear. "Hey, Mr. Roper. Let me explain what happened." Mike talked into the box for a long time, telling it what had happened that day. Finally, he ended it by saying, "Absolutely, I will call you before anything like this happens again. Thanks for understanding."

Mike dropped onto the couch and let out a big sigh. "Well,

Coco, I almost lost my job for you. I hope you appreciate it, girl." He picked me up and scratched my neck just the way I liked it. "I guess it's going to be you and me now. The two amigos. Is that alright with you?"

I barked loudly at him. That sounded great to me.

That day I learned that doing the right thing might be risky sometimes, but worth it in the end.

NOVEMBER 29

CELIA CAME every afternoon to take care of the horses. It was hard to tell if she was like Miss Loretta, or like Lillian. I tried to jump on her to say hi, but she would always say "down girl," and walk straight to the horses. They weren't very pretty horses. I don't know why she liked them so much. Mike would always ask her if she wanted lunch, but she would say, "No, I'll eat at work." I didn't like that. Mike already told me he had a hard time talking to people.

Mike talked about Celia to me a lot, telling me how hard-working she was, how she never complained, and how "gorgeous" she was, even though I didn't know what that meant. He looked at her a lot too and tried to help her with the horses even though she said she didn't need help. One day, he gave her a little glittery bag with paper sticking out of the top.

"What's this?" Celia asked with a scrunched-up face.

"You've been super patient with me the last couple of months while I've been figuring this place out. It's just a little thank you gift."

"I haven't been patient with you at all."

"Yeah, I guess you're right. Still, thanks." Mike quickly turned and walked out of the barn. I stayed to see what Celia thought of his gift. He was very nervous to give it to her. I know because he told me so. She could have at least said thank you.

She sat on a bale of hay and stared at the bag. "What in the world?" she said to herself. She never talked to me.

Slowly, she pulled out the things in the bag. It was a big bag of gum, the kind she always chewed, a shiny mug with a horse on it, and a pair of earbuds with a note attached. She opened the note and read, "I can put up with your God-awful singing, but that country music is another story. Thanks for making me feel at home. Love, Mike." Celia looked at the earbuds and started laughing. She laughed louder and louder until water came out of her eyes and ran down her face. I never saw anyone have watery eyes unless they were sad.

I ran out of the barn to look for Mike. He was way on the other side of the farm feeding the chickens. I jumped on him, excited to tell him the news.

"Did she like it, Coco?"

I barked loud and high. Mike chuckled. "Thank God. I knew she had a sense of humor somewhere in there."

That day I learned that humans like to give gifts to the people that make them the most nervous.

DECEMBER 7

EVERY DAY the air got colder. I liked it because my barks looked like smoke in the air. I started to figure out where the sun was in the sky when Amelia came on the big bus. It was the best part of my day. I loved Mike, but he didn't like to play the same way that Amelia did.

One day, Amelia came off the bus slowly, and her face looked very sad. When I jumped on her and kissed her, I could taste salt on her face.

"You okay, kid?" Mike sounded as worried as I was.

"I'm fine." Amelia picked me up and ran into the barn. We sat in the corner of the barn and she buried her face into my fur. I was worried about her, so I whined. "It's okay, Coco." She pet my head softly. "I had a big show at school today. I sang a Christmas song in front of everybody. I did so good! I practiced a lot in the mirror. Mommy was there, and Nana. Even Papa and Grammy came! And she can barely walk now. But," her lip bubbled up, "my daddy didn't come."

Water came bursting from her eyes and she made loud crying sounds. I whined as loud as I could so that Mike could find us. He was a very smart man. He would know what to do.

"Amelia! What happened?"

"My daddy didn't come today! And he promised he would!"

"Aw, man. I'm sorry. That sucks." Mike sat next to us and put his arm around Amelia. "Your mom said you might be upset. She told me you did a great job. That was so brave of you to sing in front of everyone. I could never do that."

"Really?" Amelia sniffled. "But you're a grown-up."

Mike laughed. "Yeah but that's still hella scary!" Mike coughed. "I mean, really scary. You're super brave. I'm serious."

Amelia rubbed her eyes. "Thanks."

"Why don't we blow off these chores and get some ice cream?"

"Really?" Amelia brightened. I knew Mike would know what to do. "But it isn't dinner time yet. Mommy won't like that."

"Well, this is a special day, and we need to celebrate. I'm sure it'll be okay, just this once. I'll text her just to make sure. Coco," he looked right at me, "you're in charge until we get back!"

Amelia giggled at that, and it made me so happy to see her feeling better. Mike was a very special man.

I tried to watch the farm like Mike asked me to. I made my way around every couple of minutes, chasing the squirrels away and barking at the birds. I was proud that Mike asked me, and not Buster, the biggest dog on the farm. Even though Buster was the biggest, he wasn't very smart. Mike had to keep him locked up so he wouldn't run away. Mike could tell that I was trustworthy, even if I was small.

My hair stood up when I saw a car pulling up, but I soon realized it was Celia's car. I was so relieved!

She didn't usually talk to me, but this time she came right to me and picked me up.

She sat with me on the porch swing and we rocked silently for a long time. She scratched my neck just right. I was almost asleep when she started talking to me.

"I had a rough day, Coco." I looked up and saw she was frowning and had water in her eyes. I didn't know Celia could get upset. She was the toughest human I knew.

"I try to do everything right, try to give Amelia the life she deserves. It's not her fault that I got pregnant in high school. It's not her fault that she has such a terrible dad. I never would have picked him to be the father of my children. I was just a kid myself, who grew up without a dad. I hated it. And now I'm doing it to my daughter." Her voice cracked and she covered her face with her hands. I stood up and kissed her. She hugged me tightly. I was wrong about Celia. She was just as sweet and gentle as Amelia. "Thank you, Coco. I'll be okay. Thank God for Mike today. He's such a great guy." She smiled, and I wagged my tail at the mention of Mike's name. He was a great guy. "If my life was different, he would be the guy I'd go for. But I don't deserve anything like that anymore."

I barked at her in protest. What a silly thing to say!

Just then, Mike pulled up with Amelia. She ran out of the car toward me, back to her happy self. "Coco! We got you a treat! And Mommy I got you some ice…" she stopped when she saw Celia. "Mommy, what's wrong?"

"Nothing, baby! Thank you so much. Mocha Mint! My favorite!" She gave Amelia a big hug, and whispered, "Thank you" to Mike. "Did you have fun, honey?"

"Yes! Mike got me a large scoop because he said I'm a big kid now. And guess what?"

"What?"

"He's gonna take me fishing! He just has to get the supplies. He said he'll teach me!"

Celia laughed. "That sounds great! For now let's head home and get some dinner if you've got any room left in that tummy!" She tickled Amelia on the belt and made her giggle.

Celia cleared her throat and looked at Mike, "I wanted to know if you'd have dinner with us on Sunday. It'll just be my grandparents, my mom, Amelia, and me. Don't feel obligated or anything."

"I'd love to." Mike was beaming.

"Great. I'll see you later."

"Goodnight, Mr. Mike!"

"Goodnight, Amelia! Thanks for hanging with me today."

Mike watched them drive away and stared after them for a long time. He didn't talk much that night, and his face looked serious. I wondered what he was thinking.

That day I learned that you can't judge a human by what you see the first day.

DECEMBER 10

MIKE BROUGHT me to dinner that Sunday, and I had so much fun. Celia's mom was nice to me, she even gave me a little plate like a person. I ate so much my tummy hurt and lay on the couch with Amelia where she fell asleep. Mike said I could stay the night with her. I was happy I didn't have to get up.

I listened to Celia's mom sing while she and Celia cleaned up the kitchen.

"He is lovely, Celia."

"It's not like that, Mom! We just work together on Papa's farm."

"Honey, stop wasting time and snap that man up. He was making puppy dog eyes at you all night."

I wondered what she meant. Mike did have pretty eyes, but they looked like people eyes. Were puppy dog eyes good? Celia's mom made it sound like it was good.

"Is it because you have Amelia? From what Dad says, Mike has quite a checkered past himself. Besides, he's wonderful with Amelia, and she adores him!"

"I just think he deserves better."

Celia's mom crossed the room and cupped Celia's face in her hands. "You are kind, beautiful, and fierce. Any man would be lucky to have you. And if you don't hurry up and grab this man, I will."

Celia laughed at that. "Thanks, Momma. I might do it just to save him from you!"

Celia gave her mom a big hug, right before I dozed off in Amelia's arms.

That day I learned that mommas are special people.

DECEMBER 23

THE NEXT TWO weeks got cooler, and everyone seemed to be in a bright mood.

Amelia had jumped off the bus one Friday and scooped me into her arms. "It's Christmas break, Coco!" She ran around the yard whooping and laughing. "We can spend all Christmas break together. Is that okay, Mike?"

"I guess you can borrow her for a little while if it's okay with your mom."

Amelia asked as soon as her mom pulled up that evening.

"Maybe just tonight. If that's okay with you, Mike."

"Sure. I know Amelia will take good care of Coco."

"I will!"

"Are you still coming to Christmas dinner?"

"I wouldn't miss it." Mike smiled.

I had fun at Amelia's house. We put a tree inside the house! Then Amelia and Celia put glitter toys all over the tree. They told me I wasn't allowed to play with the toys, even though they put bright blinking lights all around them. I didn't mind too much. It was pretty to look at. They put boxes of all different sizes under the tree, and Amelia showed me a long stick that she was extra excited about. "This is a fishing pole for Mike! Mommy got me one, too. She said it's an early

Christmas present. And I got lots of fat worms to stick on there. Don't worry, they're fake. Do you think he'll like it?" I barked loudly. I did think he would like it.

. That day I learned that cold weather means giving people you love special presents.

DECEMBER 24

THE NEXT DAY, we drove back to Mike's. Amelia was so excited about the stick, she wanted to give it to Mike right away. When we pulled into the driveway in front of his trailer, she ran to the door even faster than I did.

Mike answered the door with a big smile. "What's this?"

"I got this for you! Mommy helped me pick it out. Do you love it?"

"Wow." Mike grabbed the stick and looked it over carefully. "This is a nice one. I can't believe you guys did this for me."

"And Mommy wrote this card for you. I don't know what it says, but she told me to give it to you. Anyways, she's waiting in the car for me. I'll see you at dinner tomorrow!" Amelia leaned down and kissed my head. "See you tomorrow, Coco! I'll miss you so, so, so much!"

After Amelia left, Mike sat on the couch and opened the card from Celia. It must have been very important because he looked at it for a long time. He kept going back and reading it again. I didn't know if it made him happy or sad because even though he gave me dinner, he forgot to get himself some.

"Coco. I need a female's perspective on this. Listen to this note. 'Dear Mike, I wanted you to know how much you've come to mean to us the last couple of months. I have a hard time trusting people, but you have been so kind and patient with me, even on my moody days. I thoroughly enjoy your company. I hope we can get to know each other better. Love, Celia.'"

Mike stared at me for a long time. I didn't know what he wanted, so I finally just barked at him.

"I know, right?! What does this mean? Does she like me? Does she just want to be friends? What?!" He groaned loudly, which startled me, and threw himself on the bed. "She's so hard to read, Coco. I *really* want to go for it, but if I'm wrong it would make working here hell. And I love this job. But if I'm right..."

He didn't finish his sentence, so I don't know what would happen if he was right. He only stared at the ceiling. "Screw it. I'm going in headfirst."

He got up and grabbed a notebook off of his desk. He spent a long, long time scribbling on papers, crumpling them up, and scribbling on more. I had a lot of fun chasing the paper balls around and tearing them into tiny pieces. After a couple of hours, he held up one of the scribbled papers and said, "Tell me what you think of this. 'Dear Celia, thanks for the fishing pole. It's probably the best gift I've ever gotten. I don't know how you feel about me, but I want you to know how I feel. The moment I met you, you knocked me off my feet. Besides the fact that you're gorgeous, you're hardworking, selfless, and the coolest horse girl I've ever met. I love watching you with Amelia. You are an incredible mom! I left a lot of crap behind me when I moved here. I definitely don't deserve to be with someone like you. If you're not interested, please don't stress about my feelings. Burn this letter, and I'll admire you from a distance. But if you do give me a chance, I promise I'll spend every day making myself worthy of you. Yours truly, Mike.'"

He stared at me for a while. I didn't know what he

wanted, and I was getting sleepy and grumpy so I growled at him.

"Don't get jealous, girl, I still love you, too." He patted and kissed my head. "There are some things you can only get from a woman though." He laughed at that. I don't know why. "This might be my chance to be happy. Let's go to bed, Coco."

That day I learned that feelings are complicated for people and can make them nervous.

I was excited to go back to Amelia's house and see all the twinkly lights everywhere. It was extra cold outside, and white dots started to fall from the sky. They were fun to jump up and bite. Mike put a big ribbon on my neck and sat me on the couch right before we left. I was worried I was in trouble for biting the white dots.

"Listen, Coco. You're going to go to Amelia's house, and you're going to stay there. You're going to be her doggy from now on."

I whined and put my paw on him.

"It's okay. I'll miss you like crazy, but she needs you right now more than I do. Besides, if I play my cards right," Mike smiled at me, "hopefully we'll be together again soon."

When we pulled up to Amelia's house, there were sparkly lights on all the bushes in front of her house, too. It looked like someone pulled the stars from the sky and sprinkled them onto the yard. I never saw anything prettier! The white stuff from the sky stayed on the ground. When I stomped on it, I sunk into it. It was so cold!

Amelia opened the door. She was wearing a very pretty dress and had big curls in her hair. It reminded me of Mike's curly hair.

"Hi, Coco. Hi, Mike. Where is my present?"

Mike laughed at her. "Right here." He handed me to Amelia, and she screamed so loud it hurt my ears.

"Really? I can keep her?"

"Only if you let me visit a lot."

"You can come every day! Thank you, thank you, thank you!"

Amelia ran to Celia, screaming, "Mike gave me Coco!"

"Is that so?" She put her hands on her hips and cocked her head at Mike.

"Yep. And this is for you." He handed her a big bucket of chocolate mint ice cream and the letter he had written.

Amelia took me into her room to play, but she left the door open so I tried to keep an eye on Mike. He told me in the car that he was worried about what Celia would think of his scribbled paper. I hope she liked it. He worked very hard on it.

She stared at it for a long time, the way that he had looked at hers. Finally, she looked up with water in her eyes. I thought this was a bad sign, but then she walked right up to Mike and kissed him on the mouth! I never saw humans do that before. I wondered if I should save Mike, but he wrapped his arms around her waist and kissed her back. I guess humans liked to kiss on the mouth after all. They stood like that for a while, then pulled away and gave each other a hug. I could see a big smile on Mike's face. I never saw him look so happy.

The rest of the day was magical. I got lots of toys and got to rip up lots of papers. Amelia and I played until we both ran out of energy, and I fell asleep on her bed.

That day was my favorite day because that day I learned that Christmas means family.

THE END

A SURPRISE FOR CHRISTMAS

BY PATRICIA WILSON

A SURPRISE FOR CHRISTMAS

JULES BARELY MADE it to her cell phone, and when she picked up, she heard silence at the other end.

"Hello? Hello?" Holding the phone in the crook of her neck, she wiped shampoo and water from her hands with the green towel hanging over the side of the tub.

"Is this... *Dogs for Veterans*?" The voice was hesitant, as though he might hang up at any moment.

"Yes. Yes, it is." Jules desperately held Tess's leather collar with her free hand, but the big husky mix shook anyway, covering her with wet lather. "Nooo..." she moaned.

"Is everything okay, ma'am? This *is* the rescue, right?"

"Oh, yes! So sorry... I was bathing my dog and she just sprayed me with water. A lot of water."

"Maybe I should call back another time..."

"No, no. I'm fine—it's fine, I mean." She pulled together a businesslike tone. "How can I help you?"

"I think I may be interested in adopting a dog."

"Well, we can certainly help you there." Jules adjusted the phone against her shoulder and toweled off the wet dog as best she could. Tucker, a blue heeler, watched curiously, cocking his head to one side. "I'm Jules Murphy, by the way."

"Are you the owner?"

27

"*Dogs for Veterans* is a non-profit, but I am the CEO if you could call it that. I have a lot of help from our volunteers and fosters."

"I'm John Stanton. I'm not really sure what I want… just a good dog."

"Well, Mr. Stanton, why don't you make an appointment to come by and we can arrange to meet our available dogs? I'd be happy to tell you about each one we have and find out a bit more about what you are looking for."

"That sounds good." His voice was still hesitant.

"Of course, there would be no obligation on your part. Just come check us out. If our rescue doesn't have what you need, I can give you plenty of recommendations. How about this Saturday?" Three days should give her enough time to make arrangements with the other foster parents.

"Does Saturday at eleven o'clock work?" He sounded a bit more certain.

"Perfect! I'll text you the address and e-mail you an application to fill out. We will need three references. If you do decide to adopt one of our dogs, the fee is one-hundred-fifty dollars."

"Thanks. I'll send my e-mail address. Can I ask you a question?"

"Sure!"

"Why is it *Dogs for Veterans*? I mean, why us?"

"My dad is a retired US Marine, and my brother is in the Air Force. I discovered that there was a real need to help our ex-military. Dogs can help in so many ways, from situations such as PTSD to the loneliness a veteran might experience after separation. Our dogs are all solid companions, with basic obedience training and intensive evaluation. We also foster dogs for military personnel who are deployed, and have no other options to care for them."

"That's a great service. I know a lot of guys that worry about that scenario. I'll see you Saturday."

"See you then, Mr. Stanton." She heard a click at the other end.

"Hey, girl," Jules said excitedly, putting down the phone, and picking up the towel again. She did a little happy dance.

"Did you hear? Did you? Yay, yay, hooray!"

Tess jumped up enthusiastically, and Jules took her by the paws, doing a little waltz in a circle. Tucker followed them around, growling playfully.

"One of your buddies might get a home!"

*S*aturday, Jules took the luxury of sleeping in a bit— at least, until four dogs converged on her, demanding breakfast with whining and the poke of cold noses. Grumbling, she rose and threw on a plaid flannel robe.

After portioning out kibble and a bit of canned food in each bowl, she spaced them out on the kitchen floor and stood guard while the dogs ate to make sure there were no squabbles. She glanced over at Finn, the newest rescue. He was still lying on his bed in the mudroom, last night's food barely touched. When the dogs finished, she escorted them outside. Finn remained behind, and Jules guessed he had used the doggie door earlier. The terrier mix showed no interest in mingling with the others.

Standing in her generous backyard, Jules shivered and stared up at the thick gray sky. There was no snow yet, but the local weatherman in Middleburg, Virginia had predicted some flurries. It would be great to have a white Christmas, but she wasn't holding her breath.

Jules's partner, Cheryl, was on her way after picking up two other fosters and promised to bring lattes and bagels by ten o'clock. Their prospective adopter would be driving over from Falls Church, less than forty-five minutes east of Middleburg.

John Stanton had e-mailed the application back to her yesterday, and everything looked good. He was twenty-seven, a single ex-Army Sergeant First Class, and owned a house with a fenced yard. She had checked out his references and gotten great feedback.

Jules ran a comb through her tousled dark hair and pulled on jeans and a navy turtleneck. She found one Blundstone leather boot and looked around the room for the other. Finally, she put her hands on her hips.

"Bruce Lee!" she called out to the pit bull. "Where are you, and where is my shoe?" The pittie ran into her bedroom, his stout brindled body wriggling in greeting.

"You goof! What did you do with it?"

The dog barked, sitting back on his haunches. Jules got on her knees to look under the bed. Bruce Lee ran over and crouched down by her side with another bark. The offending boot lay on its side. She squeezed under the bed and retrieved it, shaking the shoe at Bruce Lee, who lowered his head and refused to meet her eyes. The big lug never destroyed anything but hid any shoe he could get his paws on. Her bad for leaving them out.

When she entered the living room, Tucker was waiting by the leashes. The heeler looked expectantly for his morning walk, but today she had to disappoint him. Jules bent and rubbed the dog behind his big prick ears.

"Sorry, boy. We have a visitor coming, so show us your best behavior. Maybe Cheryl will play some ball in the back-yard with you when she gets here, hmmm?"

She lifted a tennis ball from the basket nearby, and looked over at Finn, waving it invitingly. Tess, Tucker, Bruce Lee, and Molly—a good-natured black labrador—watched, entranced.

"How about you, Finny? Are you up for some ball?" The scruffy black-and-tan terrier mix just lay there despondently. She picked up the dinner bowl.

"Oh, Finn," she sighed. "You miss your master something awful, don't you? Next time it will be your turn when you're ready, little guy."

She bent and held a dog biscuit near him, which he sniffed

and tentatively took from her hand, chewing it slowly. Not so the other three dogs, who wolfed theirs down immediately. Molly easily caught the one Jules tossed in the air.

"Good girl!" She gave them all another, but Finn looked away, refusing his.

"It's okay, Finn. You just take it easy." The dog laid his chin on his feathered paws.

Jules quickly pulled on her down jacket and ran Tess next door to her neighbors, who had kindly offered to take her for an hour or two. The big white clapboard house was heavily laden with Christmas lights. Middleburg was famous for its seasonal decorations, but between running *Dogs for Veterans* and her job, Jules rarely had time to put up anything, but she always managed wreaths at the windows and on the door of her small one-story home. She was proud to be a property owner in this beautiful little town.

Bill Jenkins opened the door before she could ring the bell.

"Hey, Jules! Hey, Tess! I'll take her. Good luck with your adopter. Fingers crossed! Carl is making cookies; I'll send some home with you when you come to pick her up."

"You guys are the best!" Jules blew him a kiss and hurried home.

Once back in her house, she brushed Molly, Bruce Lee, and Tucker until their coats gleamed. Thank goodness, the rain had stopped on Wednesday and baths were unnecessary. Her dog was the worst offender when it came to rolling around in the one muddy corner outside, but Molly came in a close second.

*A*t quarter-past ten, there was a soft knock at the door; Cheryl knew better than to hit the doorbell and solicit a cacophony of howls. As it was, Bruce Lee continued to bark loudly until Jules opened the door to admit her best friend.

Cheryl shooed the excited dogs away, balancing two

coffees and a brown paper sack. Not only was she a skilled dog trainer, but she juggled the rescue's finances and foster operations effortlessly. Jules couldn't manage without her.

"Bobby and Missy are in the van sitting in their crates. I thought we might have a minute of breakfast before bringing them in." The athletic-looking redhead set the food and drinks on the countertop.

"Hi, guys and girls! Can you sit for me?" The dogs looked up attentively as Cheryl gave the "sit" signal, each one lowering their haunches to the floor obediently. She released them with lavish praise.

"What good dogs! Is one of you going to find a home today? Are you? I sure hope so!" She glanced over at Finn, still in his bed. "No change yet, huh?"

Jules shook her head. "No. But it's only been three weeks. It's just going to take a while. He's been great… gets along with everyone, perfect in the house, smart—just depressed. Aren't you, sweet boy?" she crooned at him. Finn's folded ears moved, but the terrier remained where he was.

Cheryl shed her coat and scarf, while Jules unwrapped the bagels and set down a small tub of cream cheese from the bag. "Cinnamon raisin! Yay!"

"You don't think I know your tastes by now?" Cheryl grinned. The girls shared a room as freshmen at Sweet Briar College and had remained tight ever since. "Where's Tess?"

Jules bit into the crusty bagel smeared with hazelnut cream cheese. "Oh, my God," she moaned. "Sooo good. I took her next door to Bill and Carl's. They said they'd keep her. I figured it would make things easier to have her out of the way."

"Did they say anything about the wedding?"

"Yep. It's in February. Valentine's Day."

"Awww! We'll have to think of a great gift." Cheryl finished her sesame bagel and took a sip of latte. "So, tell me about our prospective owner."

Jules shrugged. "We didn't talk too long, but everything

seems good on paper. He's ex-Army, medically discharged a year ago. He had dogs when he was a kid, but none since adulthood. Under the 'why would you like one of our dogs' section, he just put companionship. John Stanton seemed nice enough on the phone, just a bit unsure about the process. I told him it was a meet and greet with no strings attached."

"Sounds good! I guess I'd better bring in the others."

While Cheryl was outside, Jules cleared away the breakfast debris and took a last look in the bathroom mirror. A tallish twenty-something girl with a short mop of dark brown hair, a few freckles, and a generous mouth stared back.

"Okay, Jules... you got this. Just relax and let it happen." Prospective adopter visits always made her a bit anxious... it was hard not to show how badly she wanted something to work out.

Cheryl came back in with Bobby, a long-haired retriever something, and Missy, a Jack Russell terrier. Both came from outside foster homes. *Dogs for Veterans* had five people on call, each prepared to take one to three dogs. Right now, the rescue sponsored six foster dogs in different homes, all in various stages of training and evaluation. Missy and Bobby were the two most ready for adoption.

While Cheryl settled the dogs and put them through basic commands, Jules arranged the information packets. She double-checked each folder for pictures and the dog's history, a breed information sheet, personality description, and certificate of training. A few had AKC papers as well.

At ten to eleven, Cheryl suggested she take the dogs outside to wait. "Just close up the doggie door behind me."

Jules looked doubtful. "It's pretty darn cold out there... won't you freeze?"

The other girl was already putting on her coat and gloves. "Nah. It will be better if they don't bombard him all at once. And it will give you a few minutes to talk. Just come call me when you're ready." She wrapped a long, knitted scarf around her neck and grabbed a couple of tennis balls.

When Cheryl and the pack went into the backyard, Jules added some water to the tray under her Christmas tree. She found a great blue spruce this year, and the pungent aroma of pine filled the air. Dad and Mom's gifts were laid out underneath the tree; she had received them a month ago, even though Christmas wasn't for another sixteen days. Jules smiled—her dad the Marine, always ahead of schedule.

There were a few other gifts as well from friends or coworkers, but anyone close to Jules knew she hoped for donations to the rescue. This was *Dogs for Veterans's* big season; December and January gifts usually carried them through the rest of the year. She was lucky to have her job as a riding instructor at a local horse show stable for extra income. But dog food, supplies, and veterinary care added up quickly, and it seemed *Dogs for Veterans* barely kept their heads above water, even with donations and adoption fees. Cheryl worked as a tech in a veterinary practice outside her dog training business and, luckily, Dr. Rierson was great about offering free spays and neuters to the rescue, as well as discounted services.

*A*t eleven o'clock on the dot, the doorbell rang. Jules opened up the door. The figure outside wore a military camouflage jacket with a black wool scarf wrapped around his neck, and a dark green watch cap.

"Mr. Stanton?" The name was velcroed above the right breast pocket of his jacket. "Come on in. I'm Jules Murphy."

"John Stanton." He entered, stamping his feet on the welcome mat, and held out a hand. His handshake was firm and warm.

"Can I take your jacket? The dogs are outside with my business partner, but we'll bring them in shortly."

John took off cap and gloves, stuffing them into his pockets, and shrugged out of the coat, handing it to Jules with the scarf. "I believe we'll be getting some snow after all."

His voice was pleasant, with just the hint of a New England accent. Jules took a good look at the veteran. He was taller than she was by a good two or three inches, with short sandy-blond hair, and light eyes—gray or blue, or something in-between—creased by the sun. Under the long-sleeved t-shirt he wore, it looked like he worked out... *a lot.*

Mindful of Cheryl outside, Jules hurried things along. "Thanks for the application. Everything looks great. Have a seat, and let me get Cheryl." Jules indicated the comfortably worn leather sofa, and he sat down. She opened the back door and stuck her head out. "Hey, Cher! Come on in and meet John. The dogs will be okay outside for a bit."

Three furry heads poked in the crack of the door just before it closed, and Jules pushed them back outside, laughing. "Not yet, guys!"

Cheryl squeezed in with a firm "Back!" to the dogs and quickly shut the door. "Whew!" she said, pulling off her mittens to shake John's hand. "Cheryl Francis."

He stood, and shook. "John Stanton. Pleased to meet you both, by the way. Thanks for fitting me in so close to the holidays."

Cheryl sat on the sofa beside him, and Jules took the matching leather recliner across the way.

"No problem! Mr. Stanton—" Jules began, leaning forward.

"John," he said promptly. "May I call you Jules? And Cheryl?"

"Of course," she told him. "John, what exactly are you looking for in a dog, and how would one fit into your life? We'd love to hear your expectations about ownership."

"Well." He paused a moment to think, running his fingers through his close-cropped hair. She guessed it was a familiar gesture. "I've always loved dogs, but it's been hard to justify owning one when I was active duty."

"You were deployed a lot?" Jules asked.

"I was. It wouldn't have been fair to a dog. But now that

I'm a civilian, I think it's time. I've wanted one for years. To me, a dog is the best companion you can have. I'm looking for loyalty, unconditional love, the steady company—just a good dog."

"Define 'good.'" Jules felt a pang of disappointment. If he wanted perfection, no dog would please him.

"I sure couldn't ask for too much. I have a lot of faults myself." John smiled self-consciously. He had a great smile, she thought... just the slightest bit crooked.

"I guess I'm looking for a dog to accept my shortcomings, and I'll forgive theirs. And try to bring them along right. I like that your website mentioned you put some training into all your dogs."

"That's Cheryl's job, and she is great at it. But we just get them started with the basics: sit, stay, walking calmly on a leash, socialization, housebreaking. We have a doggie door where they come and go at will, so if you don't, that's something you would need to work on."

"I could certainly install one of those. I'm pretty handy. As far as fitting into my life, I work at Walter Reed as a group therapist for servicemen with PTSD. But I only go into the office Mondays, Wednesdays, and Fridays. The rest of the week, I work from home. There's a great daycare place in Bethesda I've researched. The dog could ride into work with me and stay there while I'm at the hospital. And of course, we'd go for walks... and I love the water. Maybe go on some boat rides. Do you think that would work?"

Jules nodded. "Absolutely. I love the way you have thought everything out. So, what about personality? Anything special you are looking for? A particular breed? Size?" She was thinking Bruce Lee might be a perfect match, but she knew some people were apprehensive about pit bulls.

"Not really. We just need to have a connection. I know that will happen in time anyway, but I'd like to feel a little something first. Am I being naïve?" he asked a bit sheepishly.

"Not at all." Cheryl stood. "I wish we had a hundred

adopters like you, John. Let's meet the dogs. It will be a bit chaotic at first, I warn you. They are a lively bunch."

He held up a hand. "Wait, there's something I need to tell you both. I... have some issues I am dealing with." John's face stilled as if a curtain had been drawn across.

Jules's stomach dropped. *Oh no, what? Is he too good to be true?* She looked over at Cheryl, who sat back down, and knew she had the same thought.

John hesitated; Jules could tell it was a difficult subject to discuss. "I am dealing with PTSD myself. It's gotten a lot better than it was, but loud noises, thunderstorms, fireworks —they all bother me. I get pretty incapacitated. I'm hoping a dog will help with that, so I need a brave one. There's another thing..."

He stood and rolled up the jeans on his right side. Jules could see a metal rod above the top of his LL Bean boots. "I lost my leg in an IED explosion outside Kabul. My whole right side is... well, kind of a mess."

For the first time, Jules noticed the scarring on his right hand. He held it up, and the last two fingers were missing. "It's a good thing I'm left-handed," John said wryly. "I can't say it doesn't get me down at times, but I'm able to be pretty active with this bionic leg they gave me. I won't be saving the world anytime soon, but I do alright."

He sat again, lowering the pants legs and then looking up with a mixture of pride and uncertainty.

Jules looked over at Cheryl. Yup, her eyes were misty as well. "Let's bring the pack in."

Cheryl rose and opened the back door. Five excited dogs bounded in. They immediately ran over to John, sniffing and poking him with their noses. To Jules's relief, he merely laughed.

"Okay, okay... I guess I have some interesting smells going on here." He looked up at the girls. "I promise I put on my deodorant today."

Jules glanced up and saw Finn stirring over in the

mudroom.… darn it, she forgot to crate him! The terrier was still in his plaid bed, but looked over with interest at John's voice; maybe that was a good thing. She brought her attention back to the other rescues, who had begun to settle.

Bruce Lee and Molly lay down with their tongues lolling out, and Tucker stood by attentively. Bobby, always the most obedient, sat waiting and watching Cheryl. Missy was still running about the room.

"Sit, Missy," Jules ordered. Reluctantly, the brown and white Jack Russell obeyed.

John chuckled. "Well, I think we can rule Missy out. Cute, but too high energy for me."

"That's the breed," Cheryl sighed, scratching the dog's throat. "She needs a couple of kids to help wear her out. But people seem to love the jacks, so I brought her along."

"Now, Bobby," she pointed to the big long-haired male sitting quietly, "is very well trained. He could show obedience if you have an interest. He's five, a golden retriever mix. His owner just got posted to Japan for three years and hopes we can find a home for him. Great dog!"

John bent over to Bobby, who raised his paw in response. Solemnly, John shook with him. "Hello. You sure are handsome, but I'm looking for a bit of a loner, like me."

"Tucker is a blue heeler." Jules pointed to the merle-colored dog. "They are one-person dogs, but strong-minded. You'd need to be the one in charge."

John patted Tucker's head admiringly. "Very cool dog. I'd be a bit too laid back for what he needs, though."

"His family is heartbroken," Cheryl explained. "They just had a baby, and Tucker did *not* approve. Much too volatile a situation to risk leaving him there, I'm afraid. He's just three. Molly is the black labrador over there… six years old and a real people pleaser. She was discovered with a litter of puppies during the Houston flooding last year. We got several dogs during that disaster; Houston SPCA sent us the ones they guessed were the most suitable for soldiers."

"Hmm… labs are fine dogs…" John agreed, but not very enthusiastically.

Was this awesome guy with the wonderful home going to leave dogless, Jules wondered? It would be such a shame. She still had her trump card, the ultimate companion… Bruce Lee. The pittie rolled onto his back, all four legs straight in the air, as she pointed him out.

"Bruce Lee is an excellent—"

"Who is this guy?" John interrupted, dropping to one knee beside Finn. "Hey, fella."

Jules and Cheryl stared in astonishment. The terrier looked up expectantly. He bumped John's hand with his nose, asking to be petted. John's good hand stroked his head, and Finn never took his eyes off the man's face.

"What's his story?"

"It's a sad one, I'm afraid." Jules continued to watch the pair, perplexed at the dog's sudden animation. "Finn came to us three weeks ago. His owner was on a helicopter mission in the mountains near Bagram and crashed. He never came home. The neighbor who was watching the dog called us for help. She told us he was about four; a stray from a small town in Oklahoma near where the pilot was first stationed. Finn must have been very close to his serviceman because we haven't made very much progress resettling him. He just mopes in his bed and watches the door."

John reached down to pick the dog up.

"He doesn't like that, John—he might snap at you," Cheryl warned. To both the girls' surprise, Finn stood on his hind legs, allowing John to take him. He settled in close, and draped his paws over John's bad arm, gently licking the knuckles of his damaged hand.

"This is the one," John said quietly.

"We don't know much about him. I can't guarantee anything about his behavior," Cheryl objected.

"It doesn't matter. We understand each other. Right,

Finn?" John bent his head and kissed the dog tenderly. "He's thin under all that wiry hair."

"Yes, he weighs about fifteen pounds, but he could easily gain three or four more. He's not a very good eater."

"That's got to change, okay, boy? Who heard of a pair of bachelors who don't like to eat?" Finn licked his ear. Smiling, John put the dog down, and Finn stood at his side, wagging his long, rather scrawny tail. "What kind of dog is he? A mix? He's got great eyes."

"Schnauzer, we think, and some kind of terrier," Jules guessed. "That breed tends to have large, round eyes, and a long-legged body like Finn's. He's almost got a mohawk along his back where the fur sticks up, doesn't he? And those crazy hairs going every which way around his face are kind of special, too."

"He is one scruffy fellow. I bet the girls in my neighborhood will go wild for him when we walk," John chuckled.

Jules nodded when she met Cheryl's eyes, seeing the answer to her unspoken question. "Okay, John. If you will be patient and promise not to push him, we'll allow the adoption. Finn is microchipped, up-to-date on all vaccines, and on heartworm preventative. We have a packet for you with all that information."

"I'd be happy to throw in some basic obedience training at no charge," Cheryl offered. "One of us makes a home visit anyway a few weeks after the adoption, just to check and see how things are going."

"That would be great. So, we complete the paperwork, and I can take him? That is so awesome." John grinned down at Finn. "You're going home with me, slim. We'll stop at the pet store on the way home and get everything he needs. You'll have to give me a list. Oh, and what dog food he gets, too."

"We have all that." Jules nodded. "He comes with a collar and leash, and our dogs are microchipped. Part of the adoption agreement is that we will take him back at *any* time if things aren't working, and you have my number if there are questions or concerns. Keeping tabs on our dogs and following through is very important to the rescue."

"I appreciate that. I'm sure I'll need some advice along the way. Right, boy?" Finn looked up adoringly.

"I have never seen a dog bond so quickly; especially one we haven't had luck with ourselves," Jules said in wonder.

John shrugged. "Maybe I remind him of the guy before me. I'm sure there are some similarities. Or maybe he prefers men." He flashed that devastating grin, and Jules felt a little weak in the knees.

It had been a long time since Jules had even thought of romance. Her last relationship had ended two years ago, and badly. Brad had been resentful of any time she spent with the rescue *and* her close friendship with Cheryl. It had put her off men and dating but good.

"Let's close this deal," she said with a smile.

*E*xactly two weeks later, Jules picked up the phone and saw an incoming call from John's number. She answered immediately.

"Hey, John! Is everything okay with you and Finn?"

"Just great! Didn't mean to worry you, Jules."

She sighed in relief. "No problem. It's good to hear from you." John had been on her mind ever since the adoption, and not just for professional reasons. Something about the ex-soldier reached out to her; she was deeply attracted to him.

"I hate to bother you two days before Christmas, Jules... but I was wondering about that home visit. Would you like to come by? Or if that's too much trouble, maybe we could meet halfway? There's a great coffee shop in Fairfax that's dog-friendly."

"Well, Cheryl is out of town visiting her brother, so you might want to wait until—"

"That's no problem… Finn and I really want to see you, if that's okay. What do you think?"

She was intrigued. "John, are you asking me out on a date?"

There was a moment of silence at the other end, and then a hesitant chuckle. "I guess I am. Trust you to cut to the heart of the matter, Jules."

She was not naïve; a man who had lived through John's trauma would have emotional scars as well as his physical ones. But his courage and optimism impressed her, and she appreciated his wry sense of humor, too.

"I'd love to hang with you both again," she said quickly. "How is one o'clock? If you text me the name of the coffee shop, I'll meet you there." As much as she'd love to see his home, neutral territory was probably best. There was no question of her physical attraction.

She couldn't tamp down the fluttering in her belly. She had a small Christmas gift for him, and this solved the dilemma of finding a way to reach out.

"Great!" He sounded relieved, and she smiled. Trust a guy to take the roundabout way.

"Thanks, John… I'll see you at one."

Tess nudged Jules's arm with her cold, wet nose, as Jules laid the phone down on the counter, and whined. The dog could sense her excitement.

"Hey, girl! What's your opinion? Is your mom a mess to keep thinking about a man she met once, or what?"

Tess barked sharply, and Bruce Lee bounded in to check out the fuss. Molly was already laying at Jules's feet, eyeing the English muffin she had left half-eaten. Tucker held his customary post at the big bay window, intent on watching the squirrels frolicking outside.

· · ·

*L*ater, Jules dressed with more care than usual. As she spent most of her time around dogs, or at the barn, she tended to favor denim and flannels.

Oh, crap! The barn! She had a few riding lessons scheduled this afternoon. In her excitement at seeing John again, work had completely slipped her mind. The cover of snow Middleburg had received last weekend hung around stubbornly, but Serendipity Farm was open, business as usual.

Quickly, she rang the owner.

"Hey, Laura! I was wondering if there's any way someone could cover my lessons at two and three today. Something came up with the rescue."

"That won't be a problem; we've had several cancellations with the holiday right around the corner. I can give them to Grace, she's here this afternoon."

"Thanks! You're the best! And Merry Christmas."

"You too, Jules."

She picked out a soft blue sweater to wear over a white turtleneck, her favorite jeans, and some warm woolen socks. After stripping off her flannel nightgown, Jules hit the shower. She stood under the scalding hot water, liberally applied a tropical-scented liquid soap, and burst into a hearty rendition of "Have a Holly Jolly Christmas." She didn't possess much of a voice, but that never stopped Jules from belting out her favorite songs in the shower, or while driving.

As she slipped into her clothes, Jules contemplated wearing some earrings, or maybe a turquoise pendant. In the end, she just fastened a silver horseshoe bracelet next to her vintage Rolex. The watch was her most cherished possession; a gift from Mom and Dad on her sixteenth birthday.

She polished her leather paddock boots to a deep shine before pulling them on, then sat down to finish some paperwork for the rescue. Jules made a few important calls to prospective adopters and checked in on her fosters. Then she got up and stretched, whistling to the dogs, and took them out in the yard for a quick romp. Herding everyone back inside, she turned the television to *Law and Order* to keep the dogs company and headed out to the RAV4 parked in her detached garage.

Jules drove the thirty-five minutes into Fairfax giddy with excitement. Her GPS led right to Aspen Coffee on Main Street in the middle of a picturesque downtown decorated with red bows and garlands wrapped around the streetlamps. She found a parking spot just a block away and parallel-parked the Toyota, then started walking down the street. The small Christmas package, wrapped in bright paper, was out of sight in her leather satchel.

She saw John sitting at the back of the coffee shop as soon as she entered. Jules admired his rugged good looks. He stood as she approached the table. Finn, lying at his feet, rose also, tail wagging.

"Hello, Jules. It's great to see you." To her surprise, he gave her a quick hug. His tall body was warm and strong, and he smelled faintly of a cedar aftershave. "Let me take your coat."

She shrugged out of her down jacket and handed it to him.

John looked down at Finn. "Sit." The scruffy black-and-tan terrier lowered his haunches obediently, staring intently at his new owner.

John gave a hand signal to the dog. "Stay, Finn."

He walked over to a coat rack, hanging up her coat, and removed his leather jacket, placing it on the next hook. Jules wondered if John had thought about his outfit, too; the rich brown leather coat was a far cry from his military jacket. Underneath, he wore a moss-green crewneck sweater that complemented his sandy hair and light eyes. A quiver worked its way down her spine. Jules pulled out a chair from the rustic wooden table and sat down. John sat opposite her, and a server came over to take their order. He motioned to Jules to go first.

"I'll have a latte with an extra shot," she said to the young woman.

"Just coffee for me. And one of your blueberry scones. Would you like one, Jules? They're pretty decadent."

"Sure."

"Two, then."

The server left. Jules looked over at Finn, still sitting. "John, it makes my heart happy to see this—he looks and acts like a different dog."

John reddened faintly at the praise, and her stomach did a slow flip.

"I didn't do much. Just made him feel safe and wanted. He's such a great dog... he was missing his soldier, that's all."

"That reminds me..." Jules dug in her bag for the gift she brought and put it on the table in front of him.

"What's this?"

"A little something for you and Finn. Open it."

John quickly unwrapped the package.

Strange, she had totally forgotten his injured hand with its missing fingers. Her gift was a small box, holding a brightly colored enamel coin the size of a silver dollar.

John looked up. "This is the helicopter pilot's coin?"

"Yes." Jules couldn't hide her grin. "I contacted his commanding officer, and he sent it to me once he heard the story."

John turned the piece over. "It's his squadron RMO from Afghanistan."

She nodded. "The last duty station. His name was Captain Mark Wilson. I thought you and Finn might like to have it. I think he's looking down on you both, so grateful and happy that Finn is loved. I believe that, John."

He looked up in wonder. "That's my biggest hope. Well, one of them anyway... I think you know the other." He smiled crookedly.

It was her turn to blush. *Could it be true? Was he as attracted to her as she was to him?* Jules felt lightheaded.

"Jules, the last thing on my mind was meeting someone. It just wasn't on my radar. My life has been so tumultuous these last two years… and I never thought… well, it's not an easy thing for a woman to live with this." He gestured to his leg.

"Or this…" John pushed up his right sleeve, and Jules saw the horrific crisscross pattern of scars on his arm.

"That's just crap," she said quietly. "People should be able to see beyond those. Your injuries don't define you, John."

"I'm afraid they did, for too long."

He rolled the sweater quickly down as the server approached with their coffees. She set the cups down, with two scones and some napkins.

They each took a sip, enjoying a comfortable silence. Jules appreciated that.

John slipped the coin into his pocket. "You couldn't have picked anything better. Finn and I will treasure it. But I didn't bring anything for you, Jules…"

"That is so not true!" She smiled at him. "Seeing Finn like this is a dream come true. He was just a shell of a dog when he was at the rescue. I think your bond is really special."

"Don't I know it! Right, fella?" Finn whined and placed his paws on John's leg. "We two bruised and battered soldiers need each other."

"You are not!" Without thinking, Jules slapped John play-fully on the arm. *His right arm.* She looked up, horrified.

"It's okay, Jules," he said, laughing, then his expression grew serious. "It's healed, and I'm ready to move on."

John took her hands. "Would you consider seeing where that journey goes? I'd like the chance to get to know you better."

Jules squeezed back firmly in return. "You bet. There's nowhere I'd rather be."

"Jules, look outside, it's starting to snow. You know what that means, don't you?

"A white Christmas?"

"Well, that too... but new snow always requires a kiss of celebration."

"You just made that up!"

"Finn told me to do it."

John reached across the table in the crowded coffee shop and gently touched his lips to hers. Jules closed her eyes. His mouth was firm and tender, and even though this kiss was brief, it held the promise of things to come.

"Merry Christmas, Jules."

"Merry Christmas, John. It's going to be the best one *ever*!"

THE END

THE CHRISTMAS WISH

BY ANNE LUCY-SHANLEY

CHAPTER ONE

AIDEN GULPED down his mouthful of OJ and set his tumbler on the table with an indignant clunk. "Tell her no! You promised you'd take me to the park today."

"Nancy, this is my first weekend off in a month—I'm not coming in to cover another shift at Divine Bites." Elisa Fletcher situated the phone between her ear and her shoulder, using a wooden spoon to ladle steaming oatmeal into a shallow stoneware bowl. She half-listened to her coworker, arranging slices of banana and two raisins for eyes, a strawberry for a beak, and halved kiwis for wings. "Hold on a sec, Nance."

Cell against her chest, Elisa placed the bowl in front of Aiden. She was rewarded with a grin.

"An owl!" Aiden picked up his spoon to dig in. She ruffled his shaggy coal-black curls, which were so like her own. In an exasperated tone, he objected, "Aww, Mom!"

"Eat, and I'll deal with Nancy." Elisa hurried across the tiny, cramped living room that doubled as her bedroom. The window beside the sleeper sofa led out to the old-fashioned fire escape. She set her cell down on the side table and yanked the window open. It made a ferocious shriek as the window let loose, the sash thudding as it hit the jamb. Elisa plopped down on the wide sill, her fuzzy slippers braced on the escape's metal grate. She brought her phone back to her ear. "I've already put in fifty hours this week. My feet are killing me. I need a break."

"Cynthia Birney added ham and cheese croquettes to her catering order. She loves your croquettes *and* she's a big tipper. Think of all the Christmas gifts you can buy Adam with the money," Nancy wheedled.

Elisa thought longingly of the pricey video game on her son's wish list, then straightened her spine. "His name's Aiden. And I barely recognize him these days since I never see him. The answer's no. Sorry."

"But it's so convenient with you living down the avenue."

"A little too convenient at times, if you ask me," Elisa said drily, her breath vaporizing in the nippy air. "Bethany can prepare the croquettes."

After disconnecting the call, she gathered her threadbare robe tighter and took in the early morning activity on the busy street. With few Saturdays remaining until Christmas, shoppers were out in full force. A city bus screeched to a halt at a red light a block up, the scent of exhaust and hot machinery mingling with roasting beans from the coffee shop on the ground floor of her apartment building.

Aiden, still clad in his Superman pajamas, climbed onto the sill beside Elisa and leaned into her. "Why hasn't it snowed? Santa's reindeer won't like it if there's no snow."

She wound her arm around his waist. "I'm sure it will by Christmas, kiddo."

"So you don't have to work?" At Elisa's head shake, Aiden whooped. "Then we can go to the park, right?"

Elisa hesitated. "There are errands. And we should get your hair cut..."

Aiden didn't say anything, but his face fell. Elisa remembered the heap of dirty laundry in the corner of the bathroom. There were bills to be paid and groceries to be bought. She bit her lip, meeting his hazel eyes—eyes he'd inherited from his father.

How many more days did she have before Aiden decided he was too cool to hang out with her? Until he shrugged from her embrace?

"Alright. After the market and the barbershop."

"Can I call Noah and see if he can come, too?"

"Go ahead. We can meet him and Jen." Elisa gave him her cell. "And get dressed!"

Aiden headed down the hall to his room, his voice chatty as he spoke on the phone. With a sigh, Elisa came inside and shut the window, dropping down on the sofa. Closing her eyes, she tipped her head back, considering. Yesterday was payday. If she paid her light bill late, she could probably afford the video game, and still be able to squirrel away a portion of her check into her savings account. Still, snow *would* be coming soon, and Aiden had outgrown last year's boots. Plus they had yet to buy their holiday ham.

It all took money. Despite working extra hours, there never was enough.

Aiden was such a sweet kid. Even at six he understood that she was saving to open her own business. When she'd asked for his Christmas list, there'd been pitifully little on it. Guilt sliced through Elisa. The nagging feeling was there— her biggest fear—that she was failing as a mother. She wanted so much more for her son, but things hadn't worked out the way she'd intended.

Why did you have to go and die on me, Brett? Leave me a penniless widow with an infant to raise on my own?

Aiden stood in front of her, dressed in jeans and a sweatshirt. His eyes were shining and his gapped-tooth smile was wide. "Mom, c'mon!"

With a yawn, Elisa got to her feet.

CHAPTER TWO

"How long are they going to string you along?" Jen adjusted the plaid cashmere scarf looped around her neck and fiddled with the diamond studs at her ears, her fair brow knit in sympathetic displeasure.

Elisa lifted a shoulder. Aiden and Noah chased each other around the sandbox, their jubilant laughter drifting to where she and Jen sat on a park bench. Shivering, Elisa drew the lapels of her aged woolen peacoat tighter. "Wilma's niece and a cousin are bickering over the will. The cousin thinks she wants to run the café herself."

"But you and Wilma had a verbal purchase agreement before she suffered her stroke. Doesn't that carry any weight?"

Elisa chewed on her thumbnail, brooding. The location was perfect—just outside Old Hillbury in the suburb Rockwater—where there was plenty of foot traffic. The storefronts were charming, with oodles of character. Cobblestone sidewalks and decorative wrought iron streetlamps added to the ambience. The café was nestled between a gift shop and an antique emporium—the kind of stores rich people frequented. She'd make a killing there. And the schools in Rockwater were superior to those in the city. With catering gigs in the evenings for extra cash, Elisa could swing rent for a home with a yard for Aiden. Dejected, she mumbled, "For somebody married to a lawyer, you ought to know verbal agreements mean squat. We hadn't signed a contract or anything binding."

"Hmm. I know you have your sights set on that property but maybe it's time to search for others."

"There aren't any others like that. It's special!"

"Maybe some'll come available in the spring."

"But I've already chosen the paint color—*Lazy Daisy Yellow*. I was gonna hang gingham curtains with rickrack trim on the windows. Name it after that darling film with Claudette Colbert. You know, the black and white one—*The Egg and I*. I already ordered folk art metal hens and movie posters for décor… I had so many plans."

Jen tsked in commiseration as Noah ran up to her, out of breath, Aiden on his heels. "Mommy, can we have a juice box?"

"Sure." Jen opened her designer purse, fishing out a pair of juice boxes. She inserted the straws, then handed the boxes over. The boys gulped the juice and presented her with the empties before dashing off again. Jen's sapphire eyes narrowed on Elisa. "You're exhausted, aren't you?"

"I am," Elisa admitted, raking through her black curls. "And I'm bummed about losing the café."

"You just can't catch a break, can you?" Jen played with her diamond encrusted wedding ring, avoiding Elisa's gaze. Her cheeks pinkened, but not from the cold.

"Spill it, Jen."

"Transparent, aren't I?"

"To someone who shared a foster home with you since elementary school, yes, you are," Elisa said. She studied Jen, who was like a sister, though they couldn't be more dissimilar. Jen was tiny and blonde. Pretty and feminine. She liked perfume and couture and had snagged a wealthy husband—Calhoun Blackstone Bailey—her first semester of college.

She'd become pregnant with Noah six months after Elisa learned she was expecting Aiden.

Jen was her only friend. Besides Aiden, Jen was her only *family*.

"Cal surprised us with airline tickets to The Azores at breakfast. We leave Monday morning and won't be back until after the new year."

Apprehension had Elisa's pulse racing but she tried to keep it from showing. "The Azores?"

"Islands by Portugal." Jen paused. Put immaculately manicured fingertips on Elisa's wrist. "I feel awful we won't be able to spend Christmas Day together like usual."

She brushed Jen's words away with a careless wave, though her throat ached with unshed tears. Jen had been right when she said Elisa couldn't catch a break—nothing was going her way lately. "We aren't your responsibility. I can't blame Cal for wanting to celebrate with just you three for once."

"It won't be the same without you and Aiden. I'll be missing your pecan pie, too."

Trying to shake off her melancholy, Elisa strove for indifference. "What do they eat in the Azores for the holidays anyway?"

"Your guess is as good as mine."

Elisa's attention was pulled away as she noticed an Irish setter streak across the park and leap on Aiden, knocking him to the leaf-strewn ground. With a squeak of alarm, she jumped up from the bench and sprinted toward her son.

CHAPTER THREE

ELISA FLEW TOWARD AIDEN, panic painfully constricting her sternum. Her baby was in danger!

As she approached where the dog had Aiden pinned, she was convinced she'd find her son's neck ripped to shreds and his winter coat covered in blood. To Elisa's surprise, the setter only licked Aiden's cheeks, his back end shimmying with excitement and his tail wagging. Aiden squealed and giggled, not bothering to push the dog away.

Coming to a halt, Elisa clutched her chest and took a shuddering breath. Relief flooded her bloodstream, leaving her legs shaky.

A tall man with an auburn mop of hair jogged up to her, panting. He wore an expensive-looking black parka. His breaths made little puffs of vapor in the air and he held a broken leash, his expression contrite. "I'll bet Seamus scared the bejeezus out of you. Sorry!"

Elisa glared up at the man, her knuckles planted on her hips. She was five foot six, but the man towered over her. "Yeah. I about had a coronary when I saw your mutt knock my son over."

"We were leaving the dog park," he hitched a thumb behind him, at a fenced enclosure, "and Seamus locked on him. He loves kids. When Seamus makes up his mind, there's no stoppin' him."

The man wrapped his fingers around Seamus's red-and-green-striped collar and wrestled him away from Aiden. Then, dog restrained, he extended a hand to Aiden.

Jen had joined them. She'd scooped Noah into her arms and was at Elisa's side, concern painting her features. "Everything okay?"

"I suppose so."

"Sorry, buddy," the man clapped Aiden on the back once he was on his feet, "but Seamus apparently really likes you."

"I really like him, too!" Aiden laughed, swiping at the dog drool on his chin with a mittened palm.

The man focused on Elisa, his caramel-colored eyes warm and his manner genial. "I'm Bryan Emory."

Elisa looked down at his outstretched hand, hesitated for a second, then shook it. It engulfed hers, the contact sparking awareness up her forearm. Face suffusing with heat, she broke contact and cleared her throat, wishing she'd worn gloves. "Elisa Fletcher. And this is the object of your dog's affections, my son, Aiden."

"I hope you'll allow me to buy you both a hot cocoa as an apology for my unruly dog's bad manners." Bryan's eyes crinkled as he smiled at Aiden then Elisa.

"We really shouldn't," she said, building up to casually refuse and ignoring the way his smile made her fidgety. "My to-do list is a mile long and—"

"You've got to let me make amends. My mother would be upset with me if I didn't insist."

"Nice of you to offer but…"

Bryan cajoled, "A food truck a block over serves the greatest cocoa on the planet."

"I don't think—" Elisa began.

Aiden cried, "Aww, c'mon, Mom! Hot cocoa sounds awesome." He turned to Bryan. "Can I have whipped cream and sprinkles? And a candy cane to stir it?"

"You bet, bud. The works."

Aiden aimed his imploring gaze at Elisa and she nibbled her bottom lip. Glimpsing at Jen, she discovered her friend observing the exchange with amusement. "I suppose you and Noah wouldn't care to tag along, would you?"

Over Noah's objections, Jen declared she must get to the post office before it closed. As she led him away, Jen winked at Elisa.

Elisa groaned at the mischievous gleam in her friend's eyes. *Oh wonderful.*

CHAPTER FOUR

BRYAN FIXED the leash by knotting the ends together, then clipped it on Seamus's collar. "It'll suffice 'til we get a new one. Hey, buddy, you wanna hold it?"

"Yeah!" Aiden moved to grab the leash, but Elisa stilled him.

"*You* couldn't restrain Seamus, Bryan. You really think a first-grader can hold him back if he wants to break free again?"

Bryan threw her a grin. "Seamus is infatuated. He's not going anywhere—check out how he's staring at Aiden. Total devotion."

Seamus sat obediently on his haunches at Aiden's sneakers, his tongue lolling. Elisa nodded reluctantly. "Alright. If you say so."

As they walked together down the city block, Elisa hung back, listening to Aiden and Bryan chit chat. Bryan was patient with the boy, asking him questions about school, his favorite action figures, and video games. Passersby wove around them, many loaded down with parcels and shopping bags, their steps purposeful. It reminded Elisa of the Christmas gifts she'd yet to buy. She should've refused Bryan's invitation.

Without Elisa realizing it, they'd reached the colorfully painted food truck. Three bistro tables with chairs were arranged beside it. One was empty. Bryan suggested, "Why don't you two have a seat? I'll get the drinks."

"Why are you frowning, Mom?" Aiden asked once they were seated, Seamus's leash tied on the table leg. Seamus stood at Aiden's chair, a paw on his knee.

Elisa smiled, making an effort to clear her mind. Her son deserved every iota of her attention. "I was thinking about what we're going to do for Christmas if Aunt Jen and Uncle Cal are taking Noah away for the holidays."

Aiden's bottom lip jutted out, but he stopped sulking when Bryan set oversize mugs on the table. "Wow!"

"Wow's right," Elisa murmured. Whipped cream was swirled sky high and dotted with mini chocolate morsels. Crushed peppermint candy decorated the rim, fudge sauce as glue. It dripped down the sides of the mug. A thick candy cane served as a stirrer.

Aiden took a swig, leaving a smudge of cream on his nose. Bryan laughed. He passed Aiden a paper napkin.

A dark-skinned man wearing a striped apron exited the food truck and came to them, a plastic cup of whipped cream in his fist. "Hey, Doc Bryan. Here's for Seamus."

"Thanks, Don." Bryan held the cup at an angle for the setter.

"*Doc Bryan*?" Elisa asked, a brow raised. She considered his open, sunny face, his easy smile. Bryan was cute. Little butterflies flapped their wings in her belly, leaving her jittery. Attraction—something Elisa hadn't felt in ages. Something she didn't have time or energy to entertain.

"I'm a vet. My clinic's on West Seventh."

"Ah." Elisa stirred in the whipped cream and took a tentative sip. It was delectable. She inhaled a breath, relaxing into her seat. Shafts of sunlight hit the windows on the skyscrapers around them as the sun set. The temperature was dropping. She wrapped her hands around the mug for warmth.

"So what are you asking Santa for, Aiden?" Bryan inquired, taking a bite of his candy cane.

Aiden put an index finger to his chin, contemplating. For a moment, he was silent, then his gaze fixed on Seamus. "Well, I wanted the new blaster game… but now what I want most in the world is a dog like Seamus."

Elisa's heart sank at her son's wistful expression. A dog was one Christmas wish not even Santa had the power to grant.

CHAPTER FIVE

THAT NIGHT, once Aiden was asleep, Elisa hunched over her monthly budget at the dinette. She used the calculator on her cell, her brow wrinkled as she concentrated. On the way back to their apartment, Aiden had begged her for a real Christmas tree. This year was different, he'd asserted, since they'd be staying home. Still disturbed by her son's Christmas wish and the attraction that had simmered between her and Bryan, Elisa mumbled she'd see what she could do.

Their scraggly artificial tabletop tree *had* seen better days. And learning Cal, Jen, and Noah were going out of town was depressing—shopping for and decorating a tree would lift their spirits. When the numbers scrawled on her notepad refused to cooperate, Elisa decided to forgo buying the new clothes she desperately needed. That ought to stretch the budget enough to allow for a modest tree.

With a yawn, Elisa laced her fingers behind her head, regarding the cracked kitchen ceiling. Aiden hadn't brought up the matter of a dog the rest of the evening but she dreaded explaining to him why Santa couldn't bring one. Imagining his inevitable disappointment, she sighed.

Elisa's mind strayed to earlier. To Bryan Emory. She'd been so preoccupied with how Aiden's winsome tone gnawed at her gut that when Bryan asked her questions about herself, she'd answered freely. Too freely. Telling him about her job at Divine Bites, Elisa had confided that she wanted to start her own café. Listening intently, Bryan's caramel eyes drank her in. He was friendly and down to earth. Made her pulse quicken and an arc of warmth spread across her solar plexus, triggering sensations she'd thought were long dead.

After swallowing the last of his cocoa, Aiden had piped up, enthusing that his mom was the best baker in Old Hill-bury. It was then Elisa came to her senses. What the heck was she doing telling a stranger her business? She'd reminded herself that past experience had taught her that few men could be trusted—few men were as genuine as they seemed. Brett had been an exception and even if Bryan was too, she had important goals. Ones that romantic entanglements would interfere with.

Elisa had risen to her feet. Before her son became more attached to the man *or* his dog, she'd thanked Bryan for the drinks, made their excuses, and briskly wished him a merry Christmas. Bryan had appeared thrown by her abruptness but she avoided his eyes. Hand-in-hand with Aiden, Elisa strode away. Still, her conscience had tugged at Seamus's plaintive whine as they left.

"*Mom*, time to wake up!"

Elisa opened one eye. Squinted. Sun streamed through the blinds. Her voice was hoarse when she asked, "It's late, isn't it?"

Aiden wore a red sweater and jeans and carefully held a tumbler of OJ. "Eleven."

"Eleven?!" She sat up and took the tumbler from Aiden. "Why'd you let me sleep so long?"

He replied sagely, "When somebody snores as loud as you did it means they're super tired."

Elisa smothered a giggle at his solemn expression, taking a drink of juice.

"I made breakfast for myself." At her alarmed look, he put his palms up. "Just a bowl of Oat Rings. I didn't spill the milk or anything."

"My goodness," Elisa murmured. "Aren't you grown up?"

Aiden's chest puffed out. "Yep."

"Huh. You wouldn't be buttering me up about that Christmas tree, would you?"

Aiden's cheeks flushed to match his sweater.

"I thought so." Elisa chuckled. "I crunched the numbers last night. Yes, we can buy a tree today, kiddo."

Jumping up and down, Aiden punched the air.

"A *small* tree," she warned.

"Let's go right now!"

Good-naturedly, Elisa grumbled, "At least allow me to grab a cup of coffee and shower first!"

CHAPTER SIX

AN HOUR LATER, they arrived at May's Mercantile, which was three blocks from their apartment. Netting bound trees leaned against the black-painted brick storefront. Black-and-white striped awnings were above the plate-glass windows. Wreaths hung on the windows by plaid ribbon, and evergreen branches were artfully swagged, framing the door.

The door swung outward, a bell attached to it tinkling as a young couple departed. The wafting scent of cloves, cinnamon, and sugar followed them. Elisa sniffed the air with appreciation, her stomach rumbling. She held the door for Aiden. "Let's window shop."

Once inside, Aiden pointed to a hand-lettered sign on an easel. "Look, Mom. It says Santa's here today! If the line's not too long, can I talk to him?"

"Sure." Elisa glanced around the store. It was a winter wonderland. Airy, with whitewashed brick walls and an antique tin ceiling, the perimeter was lined with metal shelving displaying household décor, all Christmas themed—stacked quilts, rows of snow globes and figurines, rustic signage. A rack was stocked with tree ornaments of mind-boggling variety. It was a beautiful place—Elisa was enchanted.

Aiden led her to an arched entryway flanked on one side by a toboggan draped with ice skates and a pair of wooden skis on the other. A combination tearoom and grocery was beyond the entryway. Most of the tables were filled with diners, their conversation a loud hum reverberating through the cavernous space. The air was redolent with the perfume of tasty food.

Aiden said, "There he is!"

Santa sat on a wooden rocking chair beside a Christmas tree. A toddler was perched on his knee, a man presumably her father snapping photos with his smartphone. Aiden grabbed Elisa's wrist and pulled her over to stand in line behind a couple and their kids.

Santa's *ho ho ho* was jolly when he beckoned Aiden over for his turn. "Come tell Santa your Christmas list!"

Aiden became bashful, but he went to Santa and whispered in his ear. Elisa fished her cell from her jeans and took a picture. The lengthy discussion that ensued between Santa and Aiden was hushed, evidently serious. Aiden's face was earnest. Santa's forehead wrinkled as he listened. Was Aiden asking for a dog? Santa's eyes met Elisa's. Sentience made her gasp and her limbs tremble.

Patting Aiden on the shoulder, Santa lumbered to his feet and approached Elisa, his mouth twitching beneath the white mustache attached to a beard. "Fancy meeting you here."

Her cheeks heating, she avoided his gaze as she tucked her phone back in her pocket. The butterflies had returned to her belly and were fluttering their wings with vengeance. "I thought you were a veterinarian."

"May's my mother. I pitch in here on my days off. My twin sisters and my dad do, too."

Aiden's face screwed up in confusion as he scrutinized their interaction. "I don't understand. You're not the *real* Santa?"

Uh oh.

With a wink to Elisa, Bryan kneeled beside Aiden. "I'm

one of Santa's helpers, buddy. You can imagine how busy he is this time of year. He can't leave the North Pole this near to Christmas. But don't worry, I'll let him know what we talked about, alright?"

Aiden nodded, accepting the explanation and Elisa gave Bryan a grateful smile. She heard a *woof* and swiveled. Seamus bounded through a set of swinging doors and headed for Aiden, an older woman with Bryan's auburn hair struggling to hold onto his lead. The setter trotted with determination past tables of diners, creating a stir through the tearoom. The woman scolded, "You know you aren't supposed to be in here, Seamus!"

When the dog reached them, Aiden sank to his knees and scratched Seamus's ears, his laughter high pitched. "I missed you, too!"

Elisa pinched her lip with her teeth as she took in the joyful scene before her. Boy and dog seemed permanently bonded. No doubt Aiden would ask to visit Seamus again. How could she justify keeping them apart? That would be selfish of her, wouldn't it?

"You must be Aiden." The woman beamed, turning to Elisa. "And you're Aiden's mom. I've heard a lot about you, Elisa. I'm May."

CHAPTER SEVEN

ELISA THREW BRYAN A QUESTIONING LOOK, feeling her face tingle as her blush deepened. "Y-yes. Uh, pleasure to meet you."

Bryan got to his feet, shrugging nonchalantly. "I mentioned what happened at the park."

"Seamus adores children," May said, her canny gaze volleying between her son and Elisa, "but this level of attraction is… unusual."

Elisa's throat tightened at the innuendo. Compelled to change the subject, she was breathless when she murmured, "Your shop's lovely. I've been by countless times, always meant to check it out."

"We're here to buy a Christmas tree." Aiden stood, his palm on Seamus's head.

The corners of Bryan's eyes crinkled when he grinned. "Well, we've got plenty of 'em. It's time for my break. I'll show you—"

"Absolutely not. You've been working too hard. Lunch first," May insisted. "Why don't you two join Bryan for a bite? I've got my famous homemade beef vegetable soup today. I serve it with crusty baguette."

Elisa's stomach gurgled audibly at the thought of food and Bryan chuckled. "Good idea. My treat."

"Can we, Mom? I'm hungry!"

"You're always hungry," Elisa said drily. There was no way to gracefully decline. She knew when she was beat. Meeting Bryan's eyes, her tone firm, she added, "Lunch sounds delicious, but *I'll* pay this time."

Bryan put his hands up in a conciliatory gesture. "Can't argue with that. Why don't you two choose a seat while I put Seamus in the office and change out of this heavy suit?"

Aiden moved with eagerness as he snagged a table for them. He slipped out of his parka and draped it over the back of his chair before sitting. "Aren't we lucky we ran into Bryan and Seamus today?"

"Sure," Elisa agreed in a wry voice as she sat, "*lucky*."

Bryan, now in t-shirt and jeans that molded to his body, brought tall glasses of lemonade. He set them down on the table. "Fresh squeezed."

"What do you say?" Elisa prompted Aiden as he unwrapped straws for the drinks.

"Thanks, Bryan."

"No problem, bud. I'll be back with the soup and the bread in a jiff."

Elisa's gaze riveted to the seat of his jeans as he hurried away, her mouth becoming dry. Bryan was sweet *and* sexy—a dangerous combination. Ignoring her body's response, she took a swig of lemonade.

"This lemonade's yummy," Aiden said.

"It is." Through the serving hatch between the kitchen and dining room, Elisa's eye caught Bryan speaking to May, his head bent to hers. Elisa cautioned Aiden, "Don't get filled up on that. Save room for your lunch."

Bryan carried a tray across the tearoom and put it on the table, setting steaming bowls and a napkin-lined basket of bread and crackers in front of Elisa and Aiden. "You guys are going to love this."

Suddenly tongue-tied, Elisa busied herself with crushing crackers into her soup and taking a bite. It tasted as scrumptious as it smelled. She never should've skipped breakfast—ravenous, Elisa tucked into her lunch.

During the meal, she could feel the weight of Bryan's gaze on her, but she kept her focus on her food. She sensed he wanted to ask her why she'd left so hastily the day before but Aiden's presence prevented him from bringing it up. Instead, Bryan made small talk, sharing stories about the patients at his vet clinic. An animal lover, Aiden had plenty of questions for him.

As they finished lunch, May came through the swinging kitchen doors. She sipped from a tumbler of soda, stopping at their table. "Mind if I take a load off?"

Elisa motioned toward an empty chair. "Your soup was amazing, May. Perfect for a chilly winter day."

"Glad to hear you enjoyed it." May groaned as she sat, rubbing the bridge of her nose. "Phew. Busy day."

"I imagine the closer it gets to the holidays, the busier it'll be," Elisa said. "That's the way it is at my job."

"Yes, precisely. Each year it's harder for me to keep pace with all the demands of Christmastime." May looked fondly at her son. "However, Bryan offered a solution."

"I volunteered for more morning shifts here," Bryan explained to Elisa, "since I know Dr. Ira will be happy to take some of my appointments at the clinic until the new year when things settle down. No doubt you've got a full plate already, Elisa—"

"Allow me, son." May lasered her gaze on Elisa. "Between the special orders and stocking the grocery, baking so many pies is simply too much for me. Bryan says you're a baker... It's asking a lot of you, but I'd pay handsomely for the favor."

"Mom," Aiden said, his hazel eyes beseeching, "you'll help May out, won't you?"

CHAPTER EIGHT

THEY'D AGREED on a dozen pies delivered Mondays, Wednesdays, and Fridays. Although she had been put on the spot and wanted to beg off, Elisa knew she'd be foolish to refuse the business. With the extra cash, her and Aiden's holiday would be merrier.

Elisa had a long-standing arrangement with her boss. As long as she wasn't poaching clientele, Elisa could use the commercial kitchen whenever it was available for a nominal percentage of her takings.

Monday before the sun rose, Elisa dressed quickly, then braided her hair. Sipping from a mug of coffee, she packed Aiden's lunch in a brown bag and tucked it in his backpack, along with blueberry muffins, hard-boiled eggs, and juice boxes for their breakfast.

"Five more minutes," Aiden pleaded when she shook him awake.

"We'll be late." Elisa plucked clean clothes from the top of Aiden's dresser. "Come on. You wanted to help May, remember?"

Aiden huffed in resignation, sitting up. He blinked drowsily.

Elisa chuckled, saying gently, "I know, kiddo. Believe me.

But you can go back to sleep on the cot in the office—just like when you're too sick to go to school and I can't miss work."

Fifteen minutes later, they'd walked the two blocks to Divine Bites, Elisa dragging their wheeled grocery cart. She settled Aiden in the manager's office, shutting the light off and leaving the door cracked. She put on a hairnet, then unpacked the bags of groceries from the cart.

On today's agenda were six baked pies—three maple pecan on shortbread crust and three eggnog custard with gingerbread crust. The other half-dozen were cream pies—three candy cane dream and three chocolate mousse in a cloud.

Later, baked pies cooling on the cooktop, Elisa shaved chocolate curls on the mousse pies before boxing them. She started the dishwasher before waking Aiden. Sitting on stools at the island, they ate breakfast, the sounds of customers in the shop drifting into the kitchen.

Elisa loaded the bakery boxes in the cart before taking Aiden to school. After a quick hug, he ran to meet his friends. The kids entered the front doors just as the first bell rang. Tucking her scarf into the collar of her peacoat, Elisa examined the sky. Dreary. A snowflake hit her nose, and she hastened to drop the pies at the Mercantile before her shift.

*Y*awning, Elisa lingered in the vestibule of the school along with other parents later that afternoon. Usually, she and Aiden would hop on the subway for the quick trip uptown to drop him at Jen's brownstone so Elisa could return to work. Elisa paid Noah's au pair to watch Aiden, but she was spending December with her family in Berlin so he'd hang out with Elisa at Divine Bites.

It had snowed all day, and a layer of slushy snow blanketed the ground. A mother of one of Aiden's classmates nodded perfunctorily to Elisa from where she conversed with other moms. Elisa flashed a polite smile in return. When her son had begun kindergarten at PS 10, she'd been invited to coffee, but she always refused. Elisa didn't know how to do girl talk. She had no time or inclination to learn it either. Eventually, the women stopped asking.

The bell rang and kids flooded the halls. After a minute, Aiden located her, already in his parka and wearing the winter boots they'd purchased the afternoon before. Backpack slung over a shoulder, he tugged on his mittens. "Mom, did you see the snow?"

"Yeah, I saw it." Elisa considered her sneakers, her mouth pulling down. They were soaked. She'd have to spring for her own pair of boots soon. "C'mon, kiddo. We've got to get back to the shop so I can finish my shift."

Elisa held Aiden's mittened hand as they stood at a cross-walk waiting for the *walk* sign. Traffic inched forward, the road slickening as the temperature dropped. She took care as they made their way across the icy street.

Aiden was a chatterbox. Elisa listened with half-attention, her mind on a catering order for an office holiday party.

"I only have math homework. What's for dinner?"

"Spaghetti and meatballs."

"Yay!"

"I work 'til six tonight."

At the shop, Elisa held the alleyway entrance open for Aiden. He asked, "Was Seamus and Bryan at May's today?"

"Nope. Guess they were at the clinic."

Elisa didn't want to think about how disappointment twisted her belly when Bryan hadn't been there. She shed her peacoat and headed for the kitchen, a scowl on her lips.

CHAPTER NINE

BRYAN HADN'T BEEN at the Mercantile on Wednesday either, so when Elisa came in on Friday morning, she was startled to find him stocking shelves.

She halted, her cart bumping into her legs. As if sensing Elisa's presence, Bryan pivoted on his heel. His face lit up with a welcoming smile and he came to her. "Good morning, stranger."

"Hi." Her cheeks prickled with heat when she read the green lettering on the red apron he wore—*gingerbread kisses and holiday wishes*. Her gaze landed on his full lips. What would it be like to kiss Bryan Emory? She cleared her throat, glancing away.

"What do you have today?" he asked easily, adjusting his striped elf hat. On any other man it would look silly, but on Bryan it was cute.

"Uh, macaroon cherry, sweet potato, and bourbon-brown butter pecan."

"Sounds fantastic. I'm starving." Bryan bent, gathering an armful of bakery boxes from Elisa's cart. As he strode down the aisle to the bakery display, he asked over his shoulder, "Got a minute for a cup of coffee?"

As if no longer under her own volition, Elisa found herself saying, "Sure. I'm not due at Divine Bites until ten."

She wheeled the cart to where Bryan stacked the pie boxes. He set a pecan pie aside. "This one's mine. I gotta see if Aiden's mom really is the best baker in Old Hillbury."

Elisa threw him side-eye. Bryan only grinned. He ushered her to the same table they'd sat at on Sunday and put the pie down. "I'll be back."

She raked fingers through her black curls, asking herself out loud, "What the heck am I doing?"

Bryan brought a tray with dishes, a coffee carafe, and a canister of whipped cream. Once everything was set up, he sat in the chair across from Elisa. He gave her a pie server. "I'll pour the coffee if you cut wedges of pie. Don't be skimpy now."

"Alright."

When Elisa passed him his pie, Bryan added whipped cream then took a bite. He moaned as he chewed and her stomach somersaulted. The noises he made were almost indecent. Bryan noticed her expression and laughed. "The way to a man's heart…"

Elisa entwined her fingers in her lap, averting her gaze.

Setting his fork down, he took a drink of coffee. "What's going on, Elisa?"

She met his caramel-colored irises and swallowed hard, her food forgotten. "What do you mean?"

Bryan sighed, searching her face. "You like me. I know you do, but you can be so aloof. And the way you took off on Saturday…"

"What do you want from me, Bryan?"

He shrugged, shaking his head. "I wanna take you to dinner. Maybe dancing."

"A *date*?"

"You say that like it's a four-letter-word."

"It *is* a four-letter-word," she argued, her palms becoming damp as her anxiety hitched. "Then we go back to your place for a romp? I don't do hookups. It's not fair to make Aiden think you want anything more than that when you don't. It's not fair to *me* either."

Bryan frowned. "What makes you think I'm after a one-night-stand?" He cocked his head to the side. "Someone really hurt you, didn't they?"

"Haven't we all been hurt?" Her jaw trembled, and Elisa clamped her mouth shut.

"Elisa."

She attempted apathy, saying, "Most men are only out for one thing. Once they get it…"

"You can't think *I'm* that way? I don't play games. What you see is what you get with me."

"Be honest, Bryan. You can't seriously want to be saddled with a six year old." Elisa's tone was sharp when she asserted, "Aiden and I are a package deal."

Bryan appeared wounded. "So? I think Aiden's terrific."

"He *is* terrific, but kids tend to complicate… Look, it doesn't matter. What matters is that I don't do relationships and I don't do hookups. Period."

"Elisa—"

"I-I have too many goals that I—"

He reached for her, his gaze compassionate. "I'd never interfere with you accomplishing your goals. Your tenacity is one of the things I admire most about you."

Elisa pulled away, her frustration sparking. "Don't you get it? I don't have room in my life for you. Stop pushing!"

"I apologize," Bryan said stiffly. "I've overstepped."

Elisa was unwilling to meet his eyes. Taut silence stretched between them, regret washing over her. Clearly, she'd insulted him. Made a mess of things. Tears clogged her throat. "No. I'm the one who should apologize. You seem like a decent guy. Truly."

"Not all of us are jerks, you know? At some point, you've

got to let people in, Elisa. In the end, you're only hurting yourself if you don't."

Teardrops spilling from her eyelids, Elisa stumbled to her feet. "I-I have to leave now."

Grabbing the handle of her cart, she fled the tearoom.

CHAPTER TEN

DURING MONDAY'S DELIVERY, Bryan wasn't around. Not understanding why her relief was tinged with misery, it hit Elisa like a ton of bricks—she missed him. His cheerful, easygoing manner. The way his expression brightened when he saw her. The warm fuzzies she got when he grinned at her.

What Bryan had said nagged at her conscience. He was right, of course. Elisa knew it wasn't reasonable or fair-minded to hold him accountable for the actions of other men in her past. She couldn't deny that it was unhealthy to shut everyone out on the off-chance they may hurt her. And it wasn't a good example for Aiden, either, was it?

Elisa had discovered from a young age that people weren't altruistic—their benevolence had a price tag. Adults, kids at school. Everyone. Especially the opposite sex. Kindness was a transaction. One you didn't get for free.

Then Brett Fletcher was briefly placed in her foster home. He became her protector, her only friend besides Jen. He was her everything. They married once Elisa came of age. It was her and Brett against the world. She'd found happiness for the first time in her life. Then, Brett was diagnosed with late-stage lymphoma and there was only crushing grief and darkness... until Aiden's birth. From the moment her child had been placed in her arms, it was Aiden and Elisa against the world.

And it had been enough. But now, Bryan made Elisa wonder if she had the right to demand *more*. Did she deserve it? She wasn't sure, but she genuinely liked Bryan. Maybe it was time to open up to him. To give him a chance.

More than once, Elisa took May's business card from her wallet. Worried at the fleshy part of her cheek as she studied the digits Bryan had scrawled on the back—the number to his cell. She contemplated calling him to extend an olive branch. Saved the number to her contacts. Even toyed with inviting him for a meal.

Wednesday, she decided as she steered her cart through the dirty snow on the trip to the Mercantile, that if Bryan was there when she arrived, she'd ask him to dinner. If he were there, it would be a sign.

But Bryan *wasn't* there.

Parking her cart by the entryway, Elisa scanned the tearoom for May. She wasn't around either, but a pair of auburn-haired twins in their late twenties cleared tables, the breakfast rush apparently past. Bryan's sisters, Elisa guessed. She walked quietly up to them, not wanting to interrupt their conversation.

"Why isn't Mom baking pies anymore?" the twin with the red apron asked the other.

"Bryan wanted the job for a friend of his—a struggling single mother." She rolled her eyes. "You know how he is, always collecting strays."

Red apron twin noticed Elisa. "Oh, hi. Table for one?"

Stray, huh? Struggling? Elisa thought. She wasn't a welfare case! There was her sign from the universe about Bryan. Gritting her teeth, Elisa painted a smile on her lips. She wouldn't let them see that she'd heard them. Or that their words had cut her. "I have your pie delivery."

On her way back to work, Elisa fumed, her anger growing like a tsunami. If there was something she couldn't abide, it was being pitied. Did she convey the impression she needed charity? That she couldn't manage things on her own? Elisa's face flamed and her hands shook. So that was Bryan's deal, was it? A good-intentioned savior complex? Swoop in and save the poverty-stricken single mother and her fatherless little waif? No thank you, sir. No. Thank. You.

Elisa felt nauseous as she slammed the alley door to Divine Bites.

Nancy exited the manager's office. "Holy cow, you're green. You sick?"

"No, I'm fine—" Elisa's stomach rumbled forebodingly.

"Maybe it's that flu bug going around." Nancy commanded, "Go home."

Saliva thick on Elisa's tongue, she nodded. Her nausea obviously wasn't from being merely upset—she was ill.

A wave of dizziness came over her halfway to her apartment. Elisa slumped against a bodega, her knuckles on her forehead. It burned. She must have a fever.

She quickened her steps, unsure she'd make it home before throwing up. Shaking her head to clear it, Elisa tried to think. There was no way she'd be able to collect Aiden from school.

Noah's au pair was in Berlin. Jen was in The Azores. Elisa had nobody else to depend on.

Entering her building, she staggered up the flight of stairs to her unit. Gagging, she unlocked her apartment door and dashed to the bathroom. Elisa heaved into the toilet bowl. After, feeling wretched, she lay on the floor in the dark. The subway tile under her cheek was cool, soothing. Eyes closed, she dug in her purse.

"Bryan," Elisa croaked hoarsely when he answered her call. "I need a favor…"

CHAPTER ELEVEN

BRYAN'S KNOCK came shortly after they hung up. She hadn't locked the door upon arriving home. Weakly, she called, "Come in."

He flicked on the bathroom fixture and Elisa flinched at the bright light. "Oh my God. You look as horrible as you sounded on the phone."

"I didn't have anyone else to call," she said. "I'm sorry to bother you—"

"Shh." Bryan shucked his white lab coat, then, kneeling, he scooped her up. He carried her across the hall to Aiden's room and lay her on the bed.

Elisa's teeth chattered as she shivered.

Bryan covered her with the comforter, tucking it tight. "Be right back." He returned with a bucket and a warm washcloth. He swabbed Elisa's face and mouth and wiped at the streaks of vomit in her hair.

"I stink."

"Yep. Which school does Aiden go to?"

"PS 10 on East Fifth."

Bryan took his cell from his pocket. "I'll dial but you'll have to do the talking."

When he passed the phone over, Elisa haltingly explained

Bryan would be picking Aiden up that day. As she slipped into a fevered slumber, she was aware of Bryan placing his palm on her cheek.

The following days were a blur. At intervals, Bryan helped her sip broth, then held the bucket when she couldn't keep it down. The fever caused chills and body aches. Elisa slept for long periods of time, often plagued by nightmares, waking sweaty and disoriented. She vaguely remembered Aiden asking from the doorway if she'd survive.

"You're awake," Bryan said, leaning against the door jamb, his thumbs in his jean pockets. He wore a button up chambray shirt with the sleeves rolled and his face was stubbled with a five o'clock shadow. "Your fever must've broken."

Elisa said weakly, "I've never been so sick in my life. What time is it? What day is it? Shoot, what *year* is it?"

"It's Friday morning. Two days after you called me."

"Where's Aiden?" She started to sit up, but Bryan came to her, stilling her. "Is he sick, too?"

"No, he's at school. We've been religiously sanitizing."

"Thank goodness." Elisa relaxed against the pillow. "I suppose I should phone work."

"All taken care of. I let Divine Bites know that you're convalescing."

"You've thought of everything, haven't you?" She considered Bryan, emotion causing moisture to gather on her waterline. "So... you've nursed me? Babysat Aiden? Cooked? Cleaned?"

He shrugged a shoulder, his mouth turning up at one corner.

"For *two whole days*," she marveled.

"I was happy to do it."

A teardrop escaped Elisa's eye and tracked down her pale cheek. "But what about Seamus and the clinic? The Mercantile?"

"Seamus is with my dad. Dr. Ira's filling in at the clinic. My sisters are helping Mom. Everyone pitched in." Bryan wiped the tear from her cheek then laced his fingers with hers where her hand rested on her abdomen. "It's no big deal."

"It is. It's a huge deal. The hugest," Elisa cried. "How will I *ever* thank everyone?"

He thought for a minute. "Maybe bake them a pie? They'd love a pie."

"I'll make them a dozen pies!" Bryan passed her a tissue and Elisa blew her nose. "Boy, was I wrong about you. You've proved that beyond measure. You're really a good guy, Bryan."

"I try," he teased, squeezing her hand. "There is something we ought to discuss, Elisa. My sisters told me about a conversation you may have overheard and—"

"Oh." Elisa shook her head, eager to dismiss Bryan's concerns. "Don't worry about it. It's okay—"

"Now, listen. They feel terrible. Caroline's words were offhand, not meant to be cruel. I can only imagine what must've gone through your head."

"I was upset, thinking you saw me as a charity case. I probably overreacted," Elisa admitted, her throat aching. She cleared it before continuing, "You see, I'm self-conscious about growing up a foster kid. The last thing I want is for people to… to pity me. Or, even worse, to pity Aiden."

"I don't. We don't. I promise."

Relief flooded Elisa's bloodstream. "Really? Oh, thank God. I'd hate that."

"Understandable, but my family isn't judgmental. The more you get to know them, you'll see that."

"I believe you."

"From the moment we met, I was drawn to you, Elisa."

She fiddled with a loose thread on Aiden's comforter. "I haven't made it easy on you, have I?"

"Nope." Bryan grinned. "I tried to show my feelings by helping you, but you're prickly about accepting help."

"That's why you engineered your mom offering me the pie gig."

"Yeah." Bryan's gaze linked with hers, his eyes tender. "I know you want to make Aiden's Christmas wishes come true. I figured the extra cash would come in handy."

"Yes. I'd do anything for him. He's my world, Bryan."

"Do you know what he asked Santa for?"

Elisa shook her head, too choked up to answer.

"Every request—all of it—was for *you*. As much as Aiden wants a dog, what matters most is his mom getting *her* wishes for once. He said you always try your best and never give up but sometimes you can't hide that you're tired and sad and lonely. That you're saving money to start your café." He paused. "I tell ya, you're doin' something right with that kid, Elisa."

Elisa's heart swelled.

"He also confided that you guys don't have any holiday plans. I want you both to come with me to my folks' place in Rockwater," Bryan said earnestly, stroking her with his thumb. "We celebrate Christmas Eve with a big meal, then go caroling around the neighborhood. Later, the adults drink hot buttered rum and the kids have cocoa while watching *Miracle on 34th Street*."

"That sounds fun, but I wouldn't want to intrude..."

"You wouldn't be. I have a nephew Aiden's age who'd love the company. Seamus'll be there, too." Tucking a curl behind her ear, Bryan caressed her cheek. "I know we haven't known each other very long, but I want you and Aiden included in our holiday traditions. I care about you."

Elisa took a breath. Why was it so hard to say what was in her heart? She plunged in before she lost her nerve. "I care about you too, Bryan."

"I feel fortunate to have met you, Elisa. You're a special lady."

Elisa snorted. "Me? Special?"

"Strong. Independent. Stubborn." He smiled gently. "And beautiful."

"Not now I'm not." She laughed, then sobered, whispering, "Yes, Aiden and I would love to go to Rockwater with you Christmas Eve."

Leaning down, Bryan brought his lips to her forehead.

Even a chaste kiss had Elisa's pulse hammering with excitement. With a sigh, she wrapped her arms around him, hugging him tight. "I smell but I don't even care."

"I'm a vet—I'm used to worse, believe me." Bryan chuckled. When he eventually pulled away he said, "Oh, I almost forgot. Your phone rang yesterday. Hope you don't mind I answered it…"

"Who was it?"

"I wrote the message on the notepad in the kitchen. Lady was Wilma somebody's cousin? Something about the property being available January first?"

Elisa's lips parted, then curved into a wide smile. Despite her matted hair and fuzzy teeth, and being barely recovered from the flu, she'd never felt better. Things were finally looking up.

All her Christmas wishes were coming true.

THE END

A CANINE CHRISTMAS

BY AMBER TERRELL

CHAPTER ONE

JESS TAPPED her foot and glanced at her watch. *It's only been three minutes? It feels like an eternity.* A teenage girl with hair the shade of cotton candy placed her fourth complicated drink order to the already frazzled barista. *You've got to be kidding me.* Jess blew out an impatient breath as "The Twelve Days of Christmas" played through the overhead speakers.

The pink-haired girl wheeled around and shot Jess a dirty look, then pulled out her wallet at snail speed. Jess closed her eyes and inhaled. She could feel the anxiety building as she thought of the mile-long to-do list waiting at work. Someone behind her sang along in a deep bass tone. "Eleven pipers piping..." Jess rubbed her temples and stifled a scream.

"Miss?" The Jitterbugs barista, whose name tag read *Laken*, stared at Jess with raised eyebrows. The light glinted off the diamond stud in her small pug nose. Pink Hair had finished and stood glaring from the pickup counter.

Jess stepped forward. "Iced chai tea latte, please," she said, her tone brisk.

She moved aside, phone in hand, desperate to check her email.

A text popped up. **Jess, our 8:30 is already here and chomping at the bit. You do not want to lose this client.**

Standing near the pickup counter, Jess tapped her manicured nails against the granite surface. She snatched her drink as soon as it touched the counter, ignoring the unfastened lid. *I'll fix it in the car. I just need to get out of here.* Whirling around to flee the hateful stares, Jess slammed into a man standing too close behind her. Her drink flew into the air, splattering her crisp white shirt on the way down and puddling around her white suede Louboutin pumps.

Gasping, Jess jumped back, trying to salvage her shoes. She'd bought them on a whim six months ago after she won her first big case. She peered up at the hulk of a man towering over her five-foot-eight-inch frame.

He glared down at her, distaste apparent on his face. His light sneakers were flecked with brown. He crossed his arms, his muscles straining against the tight gray fabric of his V-neck tee. She ignored the flutter in her stomach as she met his golden eyes and took in his dark, wavy hair. The five o'clock shadow on his jawline made her a little weak in the knees.

Shaking her head to clear her thoughts, Jess grabbed a handful of napkins and dabbed at a large stain across her chest. Frowning at the mess, she bent and used more napkins to soak up as much as she could off the floor. The hulk cleared his throat, clearly waiting for something.

Straightening, Jess refused to meet his eyes again. "I don't have time for this, and frankly, I don't think this was my fault," she said to his collar. Jess reached in her purse and tossed a business card in his direction as she ran toward the exit. She didn't look back to see if he caught it.

"And a partridge in a pear tree" serenaded her out the door.

CHAPTER TWO

JESS TIGHTENED her Burberry coat around her as she stepped out of her modest SUV. At this stage in her career, it was more important to look the part inside the office. The fancy new car could wait a little longer. Most of her income went toward paying down law school loans, while the rest went toward an impressive wardrobe. Her tiny guest bedroom doubled as a makeshift closet. Jess was just another big client away from moving out of the shabby rental house in the suburbs to a trendy highrise in the middle of the city. No more early morning commutes and no more elderly neighbors spying on her comings and goings.

Thinking of her stained top, Jess grimaced. Another downside to the suburbs. There wasn't time to run home and change, so the warm coat would have to stay on.

Hurrying through the two-story glass doors, Jess admired the letters in bold silver script. The sign *Jantzen & Jennings* propelled her inside, knowing that every day she was one step closer to making junior partner. And then one day, it would read *Jantzen, Jennings, & Justice*.

She stifled a laugh as she thought about the reaction of her law school professors. On the first day of classes every semester, each professor would comment on her name as they

took roll. "Jessica Justice? You're clearly in the right place."
Then they would chuckle as though they were the first to
realize the irony.

Jess swept through the lobby of the firm where the white
leather club chairs and couches were accented with pale grays
and blues. Heels clicking against the polished limestone
floors, she hurried toward the boardroom where they ushered
in all new clients.

She gathered herself before she stepped inside. Camilla
Jantzen was already seated at the long marble table, crossing
and uncrossing her legs, a sure sign of annoyance. Camilla
and their prospective client, a Mr. Daniel Lassiter, turned
when she walked in. Camilla's silky voice attempted to
smooth over Jess's absence. "This is Jessica Justice. She graduated at the top of her class from Harvard Law, and she hasn't
lost a case yet. Her clients are her family, and Jess lives and
breathes for them." Camilla paused and waited for Jess to
interject.

"That's right, Mr. Lassiter. I am at your beck and call until
we win this trial. I will dedicate every waking moment to
making sure we get the outcome you're hoping for." Jess
flashed him a confident smile.

Mr. Lassiter turned back to Camilla. "She may be an eager
hotshot, but I don't want someone who's barely out of their
mother's womb. I want a partner to handle my case, or I'll be
going elsewhere. She's already proven that she can't be
trusted. She couldn't even show up to the meeting on time."
He looked her up and down, his eyes lingering on her spat-
tered shoes.

Jess made a show of reading her watch. "Mr. Lassiter,
forgive me, but I believe our appointment was set for 8:30
a.m. It is 8:27 a.m. I am nothing if not prompt, and I assure
you, I take my job very seriously."

Camilla shot her a warning glance.

Mr. Lassiter shook his head. "Where I come from, if you're
not twenty minutes early, you're late, and I don't appreciate

your tone, *young* lady. No, I want a partner." He crossed his arms and stuck out his lip, resembling a petulant child.

The stress of the morning came tumbling out, the heat from her coat compounding her anger. Jess drew herself to full height and straightened her shoulders. "Excuse me? I don't know if you heard what she said, but I graduated *summa cum laude* from Harvard freaking Law School." Jess pounded her fist against the table for emphasis, causing Mr. Lassiter and Camilla to jump in their seats. "I will be the youngest lawyer to ever make partner here, and you can take that to the bank."

Camilla's eyes widened as Mr. Lassiter rose from his seat. His glasses had slipped to the tip of his nose, and spittle gathered at the corners of his lips. He opened his mouth to speak, but no words came out. Pushing the unsigned contract to the middle of the table, Jess's would-be client shoved away from the table and escorted himself from the building without a sound.

Shaking with anger, Camilla leaned forward. "Jess, if Ted Jennings were here, you'd better believe you'd be walking out of here with nothing but your designer clothes and a mountain of debt. As it stands, I'm ordering you to take an unpaid sabbatical until the new year. I'll call Mr. Lassiter and tell him I'll oversee his case myself. We'll talk again in January." She held up a hand as Jess moved to protest.

"You have been under an incredible amount of stress. I told you the day we hired you this job would chew you up and spit you out if you let it. You've held up under the pressure better than anyone expected, but Jess, you need to find a life outside of work." She leaned forward and covered Jess's hand with her own, her anger seeming to dissipate. "Jess, trust me. At the end of the day, we are more than our jobs. It took me years of therapy to figure that out. I'm giving you a freebie. Now, get out of here before I change my mind."

CHAPTER THREE

JESS PACED the worn tan carpet of her living room, wondering how things had gone so wrong. *Unpaid sabbatical?* She envisioned the Tiffany necklace sitting in her virtual shopping cart. Her present to herself for signing her biggest client to date.

The thought of being trapped in the house for weeks on end was enough to send her anxiety through the roof. Jess didn't even own a TV. Other lawyers at the firm talked about binging various shows late at night, but Jess found their chatter vapid. One didn't make junior partner by worrying about who some hot doctor would hook up with next.

Looking through her closet for things to tidy up, Jess had a sudden urge to throw every pink article of clothing she owned in the trash. Instead, she changed into black leggings, tennis shoes, and an oversized soft green sweater. Pulling a cashmere beanie down over her honey-colored hair, Jess went for the first walk she'd ever taken in her small town.

According to her landlord, the town of Sutton was tight-knit, though she'd never taken the time to find out for herself. Jess followed the sidewalk that led to the center of town, ignoring the surprised greetings of her neighbors. Light traffic became heavier as she made her way to Sutherlands Street, the suburb's hub. Old brick buildings lined both sides of the street, and Christmas lights were strung between them so that they hung over the road, coloring puddles and enchanting visitors. Festive garlands were draped over every store entrance, and many windows had hand-painted murals depicting holiday scenes.

Antique stores, boutiques, and salons filled the shops, many of which had been there for generations. Jess stepped into one busy store and watched as people filled their baskets with tacky costume jewelry and garish holiday decorations. She blanched. *Is this what Camilla wants me to experience?*

Jess beat a hasty retreat, leaving the depiction of penguins on icebergs behind.

Continuing on, she saw a crowd ahead. Trying to heed the advice of the day, she surged forward and joined them, wincing each time someone brushed against her. Pushing her way to the front of the onlookers, Jess saw they were surrounding several dog crates and a large playpen of puppies. She spun around, intending to go back the other way, but a wall of people blocked the path.

Keeping her steel gray eyes straight ahead, she walked past the crates, ignoring the pleading cries and unhappy barks coming from all around her. A woman's spiel caught her ear, and Jess stopped to listen.

"These girls are sisters. They look exactly alike, but they couldn't be more different. This one here's well-behaved, easy to train, and serious as a heart attack. The other one is goofy, playful, and into everything. I can only tell them apart by their collars. We can't leave Miss Pink alone for five seconds without chaos and destruction. Miss Green, however, is going to be the top of her class in obedience school. Now, they don't have to go together, but it sure would be nice if their owners let them visit from time to time."

Jess lowered her eyes, taking in the furry being that had just been described as herself in doggy form. It was medium-sized and unassuming, with short reddish hair and a liver-colored nose. A green ribbon was tied in a bow around her neck.

The volunteer with the clipboard, a forlorn expression on her face, watched another potential adopter walk away. Jess stepped forward before she could talk herself out of it. "Ma'am? What kind of dogs are those? Can you tell me a little bit more? I heard your sister speech already."

The woman's eyes lit up. "Well, I reckon they're some kind of hunting breed mix. Vizsla? Ridgeback? It's hard to say for certain. We tried to adopt them out together for the longest time. Probably why they're still here. They're about two years old. Owner got married and had a baby, and suddenly no one had time for them anymore." The woman rolled her eyes. "Great for running, if you're into that sort of thing." The woman scanned Jess up and down with an appraising eye. "You seem like a Miss Green."

Jess felt her face flush. "Well, to be honest, I'm a complete novice when it comes to being a pet owner, so I do need a dog that is calm and intelligent. Can I see her?"

The dog sat and waited while the woman clipped on a black collar and leash. "Why don't you take her on a walk up and down the street here. Then come back and fill out all the paperwork. We give you a month's worth of obedience classes for free with the adoption." The woman's eyes twinkled.

Jess rolled the rough fibers of the nylon leash around in her hand. It felt foreign to be responsible for another living thing. She didn't even have time to remember to water a plant. *This is a stupid, irresponsible idea.*

Moving to hand the leash back, Jess felt a light tug pulling her the other way. Miss Green wanted to explore. "Fine," Jess muttered. "Five minutes of freedom and then we're done."

Miss Green stayed close to Jess's left side, never pulling too hard or lagging behind. She kept her head up, and Jess felt a kinship with her proud, regal profile. Jess bent down and pretended to tie her shoe. Miss Green sat and examined her with keen amber eyes. "Nobody wanted me either, Miss Green, but I made something of myself anyway. What do you think? Should we make it official?"

The dog proffered a paw, and Jess laughed out loud, surprising them both. "Wow, you really are a smart one." Circling back, Jess found the volunteer. "You were right. Let's do this."

CHAPTER FOUR

JESS SHUT the hatch of her SUV with her hip, her arms full of all the things a dog could ever need or want. She tucked a fuzzy doggy sweater under her chin and unlocked the front door with two free fingers. Leading her new companion inside, Jess dropped the leash and let Miss Green sniff around.

She set about clearing a corner of her bedroom for the plush cave bed the associate at the pet store had assured her she needed. It cost more than Jess spent on her very first mattress, but those amber eyes already had her bewitched. As she fussed about the house readying it for her four-legged friend, she tried name after name aloud. Miss Green didn't so much as cock an ear.

"Lady, Penny, Honey, Cocoa, Cinnamon, Ginger, Nutmeg…" Jess trailed off as her stomach growled.

"Too bad these dog treats aren't for humans," she said, laughing as Miss Green ran over to her at the mention of treats.

Jess giggled as the dog sat up and begged, her paws waving wildly to maintain her balance. Tearing open the bag of Annie's Tasty Treats, Jess smiled.

"Here you go, Annie. What do you think of that?" Jess offered the dog a bone-shaped biscuit and then ran her hands over the dog's velvety ears, receiving a dignified kiss in return. "Well, that's settled then. Good girl, Annie."

Jess rifled through the adoption papers, offers, and coupons she'd received. A bright yellow flier caught her attention. "Kris Kringle and Komet 5K," she read aloud. "Humans must be accompanied by a Kanine Kompanion. $50 entry. All proceeds benefit the Sutton Animal Rescue."

Jess chewed the inside of her cheek. December 10th was only a week away.

Setting the flier down, she walked to her guest room and stood sideways in front of the mirror. Sucking in, Jess couldn't help but notice how much weight she'd gained lately. Wining and dining prospective clients was fun, but it had not been good for her waistline. *It's been a long time since I've taken care of myself.*

She eyed a running shoe in the corner gathering dust. Shoelace hanging from her mouth, Annie dragged its mate toward her. Jess gasped, then chuckled. "Okay, Annie. You win. Again. I hope you know what we're doing."

I haven't been this out of breath since... well, I've never been this out of breath. Jess clutched her side as she slowed to a walk, the cold burning her sensitive ears from the inside out. Annie matched her pace without hesitation as Jess gulped the freezing air. Glancing down at her watch, Jess grimaced. *Thirteen-minute miles? My grandma can do that.*

"It's been a long time since my glory days running track at Harvard, Annie. Your mom used to be fast."

Annie looked up at her with a slight doggy grin on her face, as if daring Jess to prove it.

Jess took off in a sprint, feeling the weight of the world disappear as she ran. She smiled against the wind as she moved forward, pressing into the burning in her legs and lungs. "One more mile, Annie."

Jess's grin turned to laughter as Annie pointed her nose toward the dog park and increased her speed, urging Jess on.

CHAPTER FIVE

With Camilla's warning ringing in her ears, Jess stood at the starting line trying to block out the chaos. Annie sat, indifferent, as dogs sniffed and whined all around her.

Jess stretched and pulled up her socks. Her heart pounded as she waited for the signal to start. She wasn't worried about winning; she had no illusions of finishing in the top five, or even the top fifty for that matter. She just wanted to finish.

Fumbling the leash with nervous fingers, Jess dropped it in the dirt just as the starting gun fired. Dogs and runners surged forward, taking Annie with them in the melee as Jess fell to the ground.

Tears sprang to her eyes as shoes stomped on her hands, and knees slammed against her shoulders. Scrambling to stand, Jess called, "Annie! Here, girl!" She whistled, but the now-familiar liver nose did not make an appearance. Jess brushed a dirty hand across her eyes, too upset to care about the grime she knew must be on her cheeks.

A flood of relief washed over Jess as she spied Annie's familiar Sutton Animal Rescue leash wrapped around a tree trunk. Eyes blurred, she grabbed the leash and hugged Annie to her chest. Annie wriggled, trying to free herself from the suffocating grasp. Jess set her down, surprised. "Annie, you're usually such a calm girl. Did all those people scare you?" She reached down to pat Annie's head. "Poor girl. Let's go home. I'm too shaken to do anything else."

All the way home, Annie strained against the leash. Jess frowned, wondering if the stampede had scarred Annie permanently. Stomping her dirty shoes on the porch, Jess felt her pocket vibrate. There was a text from her brother, James.

Jess, call as soon as you can. Dad fell and he's on his way to the hospital.

Nerves already frazzled, Jess hurried inside to change. Annie whined as Jess held her phone in one hand and tugged on jeans with the other.

"I'm headed that way, James. I'll see you in about an hour." Jess ended the call, dread building in the pit of her stomach at the thought of seeing her dad again for the first time after their big fight years earlier.

Annie whined again, and Jess moved to let her outside. Throwing a book, snacks, and a bottle of water into her purse, Jess tried to keep the what-if scenarios at bay. She made sure Annie was settled in her bed before she dashed out the door.

*J*ess put the key in the lock, her shoulders drooping. Seeing her dad look so frail and old in his hospital gown dissolved their rift on the spot as far as she was concerned. He did not regain consciousness during her visit, and the doctors had been uncertain in their prognosis. The heaviness of all the things left unsaid had her ready to snuggle up with Annie and sleep until James's next phone call.

Swinging the door open, Jess froze in horror. Her first instinct was to call the police, but after a few seconds, she realized the destruction in her house was thanks to Annie. Leather had been stripped from a cushion of her couch, and foam littered the ground like snow. Her prized Tory Burch bag lay in tatters on the rug, and Annie sat looking at her with one Jimmy Choo heel hanging from her mouth.

Jess slid down the door frame, too emotionally spent to move. *How could I have been so wrong about a dog?*

Annie walked over, tail whipping the air, and dropped the shoe in Jess's lap. Jess's eyes widened as she caught sight of the tag on the collar. The name Hazel was engraved in the silver bone in neat block letters. The phone number underneath was unfamiliar.

"Hazel?" Jess said, overcome with astonishment. Hazel was the spitting image of Annie. She clapped a hand to her forehead. "You must be Miss Pink! You truly are a little terror."

Jess dialed the number with a shaky hand, trying to keep her anger under control. She was determined to get this fly with honey.

A deep voice answered on the third ring. "Hello?"

Jess gave a nervous cough. "Hi. I think I have your dog."

The man yawned. "No, my dog's sitting next to me on the couch."

Frowning, Jess said, "Is your dog named Hazel? Because if so, I have her right here."

She heard the jangling of a collar, then some muttering. "You're right. This is so bizarre. The dog in front of me looks just like mine, but her tag says—"

"Annie?" Jess asked hopefully.

"Well, yes, actually. This sounds like it's going to be quite a story."

Rubbing her temple, Jess said, "I'm kind of busy. Is there any chance you could come to me? And sir? Bring your wallet."

CHAPTER SIX

JESS STOOD in the middle of the wreckage and twirled her braid around her finger. *Where do I even begin?*

Shooting Hazel a withering look, she pulled the damaged cushion from the couch to see if it could be salvaged.

The doorbell rang, and Hazel's raucous barking made her jump.

Rushing to answer the door, Jess tripped on her forgotten Jimmy Choo. She managed to grab the doorknob to help break her fall, but her ankle twisted as she landed. She let out a scream of pain, and her visitor knocked on the door.

"Miss, are you alright in there?" The banging grew louder and more insistent.

She managed to hoist herself to her knees and open the door, suddenly aware of how unkempt she must seem. She stared up into the face of the man from the coffee shop and crumpled back to the ground.

Towering over her, his golden eyes were filled with concern. "Ma'am, have you been robbed?" His eyes swept the room, his dark eyebrows drawn together. "I'm going to call the police," he said, pulling his phone from the pocket of his coat.

With tremendous effort, Jess stood up, keeping the weight

off her injured ankle. She grabbed his arm. "No, don't do that. It was the dog. Your dog."

The hulk laughed, causing Jess's face to flame in anger. "This is why you told me to bring my wallet? Every idiot knows a dog has to be crated when you're not home. This is not my problem. Besides, you're the one who committed dognapping. And anyway, you still owe me for the shoes." He wiggled a foot as if she needed reminding.

Jess leaned against the door frame for support, her cheeks burning again at the word *idiot*. She sniffed and straightened to her full height, her fingernails digging into her palm.

"If you don't mind, I've got some cleaning to do. Kindly take your dog and leave."

Turning quickly, she gasped at the sharp pain that shot up her leg and blurred her vision.

Jess hobbled to the couch and sat with her head between her knees, waiting for the room to stop spinning. Annie whined softly, her soft pink tongue finding Jess's nose. Hazel jumped on the couch and licked the back of Jess's neck, her small claws needling into Jess's shoulder blades. Laughing, she sat up, her nausea gone. The pain remained.

The man stood in the doorway, watching her with a wary expression. He ran his fingers through his hair. "Listen, you're obviously in a great deal of pain. The least I can do is help you tidy up. My name is Cole, by the way."

She snorted, then sighed. The throbbing in her ankle stripped away any pride she had left. She leaned back against a decorative pillow, shaking her head in resignation as liberated feathers floated through the air. "Alright, Cole. I'll be on the couch if you need me."

CHAPTER SEVEN

JESS READJUSTED the ice pack on her ankle and took another bite of the pepperoni pizza they'd had delivered, hot cheese trailing from her mouth. Brushing her face with a napkin, she noticed Cole watching her closely, a small smile playing on his lips as he held Hazel at bay with a gentle hand.

"What?" she asked, her heart quickening as she met his gaze.

"What's a high and mighty city lawyer doing in a sleepy town like Sutton? Your wardrobe is probably worth more than that SUV in your driveway. You're a mystery, Jessica." He leaned forward and plucked a feather from her hair. Twirling it between his thumb and forefinger, he asked, "Can I take you somewhere?"

Taken aback by the abrupt shift, Jess narrowed her eyes. She probed her ankle with careful fingers. The swelling seemed to have lessened. Gesturing to her ankle, she asked, "What's so important that I need to leave my comfy—albeit destroyed—couch?" Jess's forehead creased. "And anyway, I barely know you."

Cole smiled, and the dimple in his left cheek crumpled her resolve. "It's a surprise, and I promise it will be worth it."

. . .

*S*ettled in the truck with Hazel in between them, Cole began, "When the gun went off, Hazel went absolutely nuts. I dropped her leash and lost sight of her. I ran a few feet ahead, saw her sitting off to the side of the crowd, and we finished the race together." Cole shook his head ruefully. "I should have known right away it wasn't Hazel. She was too obedient. But we finished third, even with the delay." Cole waggled his eyebrows at her, but she wasn't ready to congratulate him on her misfortune.

"If you grabbed Annie that quickly, that means we were probably only feet from each other at the race. I'm surprised I didn't notice you. I mean..." Jess trailed off and gazed out the window, coughing.

Chuckling at her obvious discomfort, Cole turned up the radio, and Jess sank into her seat, relieved at the distraction.

After stopping to drop Hazel off at Miss Priss's Posh Paws, Cole faced Jess, his eyes shining with excitement. "You ready?"

Jess shrugged, trying to hide her piqued interest. "Where are we going?"

"We're already here," Cole said, gesturing to the tan steel building adjacent to Miss Priss's.

Next to the bright oranges, pinks, and turquoises of the dog haven, Jess hadn't noticed the nondescript building. A small sign in front read **Fashion Forward.**

Grimacing, Jess asked, "You're taking me shopping? Is this a secondhand shop?" She wrinkled her nose.

Cole grinned. "Not quite. This is my baby. I run a nonprofit for young men and women aging out of the foster care system. We take in new and used professional clothes so that they can feel confident going into interviews. We coach them on how to respond to possible questions, and we partner with local businesses for internships." His smile faltered, and he rubbed his chin. "I hate that we need to exist, but…" He angled away from her, and the unspoken words cut through Jess's heart.

Jess grabbed his hand then dropped it. She could feel the color creeping up her neck. "I'm sorry. I think it's an incredible idea. I wish this had been around when I was younger." Cole turned his soft, understanding gaze on her. The words tumbled out of her. Words she had never said to anyone. "My dad was in and out of prison from the time I was thirteen. My mom left, and I was placed in foster care more times than I care to admit. On my eighteenth birthday, my final foster family kicked me out. They kept just about every possession I ever owned. Said I owed them." The bitterness she felt was impossible to hide.

Cole took her hand, and he didn't let go. He led her toward the building, his quiet, strong presence somehow soothing in an instant what had festered for years.

"My high school guidance counselor took me in. Mrs. Miller championed me all through high school, and she encouraged me during my undergrad degree. She helped me ace my LSATs, and I know she had a hand in my interview at Harvard Law." She stopped as they reached the threshold and squeezed his hand. "This is really great, Cole."

The doors swung open, and a young woman squealed, "Cole, you're here." She gave Jess the once-over. "You're obviously not right out of high school."

"Halle, be nice," Cole said, trying to keep the laughter from his voice.

Halle just shrugged, her long black braids whipping around as she went back inside. "Cole, let me show her around. It's been so slow today. I'm bored. Go next door and give us some girl time."

Jess flashed Cole a wide-eyed *Help me!* look.

He bit his lip, his eyes twinkling. "That's a great idea, Halle. Be back in a bit." Cole's jovial tones echoed through the large open room as he hustled out the door.

Halle nodded at Jess knowingly. "He looks good coming and going, doesn't he, girl?"

Jess fought against a reaction, the corner of her mouth twitching. She gave a noncommittal shrug.

Halle plowed ahead. "Cole's never brought a woman here before. He must really like you. How long you been dating?"

The question caught Jess off guard. *Have I only known him a few hours? It feels like months.* Changing the subject, she asked, "Why would he go next door? He just ran in and dropped Hazel off a few minutes ago."

Halle tilted her head. "Wait, you don't know? He didn't tell you? He owns Miss Priss."

"What? He owns Miss Priss? But... they're all over the northeast." Eyes widening, Jess held onto a rack of suit jackets for support.

"So what, girl. He doesn't act like those snobby rich families I've lived with who act like they're doin' me a favor. Saving me from myself." Halle busied herself straightening neck ties. "He don't treat me any different. Cole cares about every kid that sets foot in here. He ain't fake."

Jess wandered across the concrete floor, maneuvering around displays of pantsuits, heels, and undergarments. She fingered the cheap cotton cloth of a pair of pants and thought of her own closet full of silk and cashmere. Guilt stabbed at her heart.

Cole's frame filled the doorway as he walked back inside. "Hazel's in timeout for destroying another doggy bed." He approached Jess, his hands clasped together. "You sure you don't want to trade?" He gave a beseeching grin. "I'll give you free doggy-care for life."

Jess pushed the shame away and laughed. "Nope, I'm good." Halle grinned behind them as Jess grabbed Cole in an impromptu hug. "This place is amazing, Cole. I love it." She expected him to release her right away, but instead, he tightened his hold. Jess felt the stress drain from her body, and she laid her head on his shoulder. Forgetting where they were for a moment, she pulled away when the door opened again.

"Hey, Braxton. C'mon in." Cole waved a broad-shouldered young man in a Sutton High football jersey inside. "Interview tomorrow at one, right? Over at Hank's Hardware?" Cole winked at Halle. "Halle here would be happy to get you all set up."

Jess was surprised to see Halle's face flush. The girl seemed unflappable. Halle mouthed, "Get lost," and Cole and Jess made a hasty exit, managing to save their laughter until they reached his truck.

As they drove back to Jess's house, she couldn't help but stare at him in admiration. "Halle is pretty fond of you. She made you sound like a superhero."

Cole smirked. "Well, I do have a giant S tattooed on my chest, but that's where the similarity ends." His voice became serious. "I was lucky enough to be taken in by an amazing family when my parents were killed by a drunk driver. The family lived on a farm, and they had more animals than I could count. They took in strays of all kinds and nursed them back to health. I got my love of animals from them." He paused, looking lost in the memories. "When I was sixteen, a German shepherd ran out in front of my car. It was late, and the road was pitch black. I never saw her. I clipped her leg, and she went down. I brought her home and nursed her back to health. She was my shadow until she died." He turned to Jess. "Care to guess her name?"

"Miss Priss?"

"You got it. Thankfully, my parents left me a sizable amount of money in a trust, and I was able to start Miss Priss at the ripe old age of twenty-two. I got in on the ground floor of doggy daycares, pet spas, and the like. My first one was up in New York, and the rich business execs and celebrities went crazy for it." He chuckled. "I got lucky. The right time, place, and clientele, and here we are. Fifteen locations and counting."

"How many Fashion Forward spots do you have?" Jess asked, her admiration for Cole growing by the minute.

"Well, that's a bit trickier. All of my warehouses are run by volunteers. It's hard to find people willing to recruit workers, advertise, make schedules, and everything else for free. Any money we get goes back to the kids we're trying to help." He made a left turn onto Jess's street. "I'm trying to expand, but it's been rough. Altruism isn't as common as one might think."

Jess grimaced and raised her hand. "Guilty. I'm ashamed to admit that I haven't been thinking of anyone but myself lately. I think I'm ready to change that."

CHAPTER EIGHT

J ESS'S LEGS trembled as if she were walking through the heavy glass doors for her first interview all over again. If Camilla had been surprised at Jess's request for an impromptu meeting, she hadn't expressed it over the phone.

Sitting down to wait, Jess took in her surroundings, keenly aware that it may be the last time she walked through the doors of *Jantzen & Jennings*. The nostalgia and longing she expected to feel as she watched the comings and goings of paralegals and clients didn't come.

Hearing the trademark quick cadence of Camilla's heels approaching brought Jess to her feet.

"Jess, you look lovely! The rest has been good for you, I see." Camilla embraced her in a quick hug, the familiar vanilla musk of her perfume doing nothing to dissipate the knot in Jess's throat. Leaving behind another mentor would be the hardest part.

She followed Camilla into her office. The gorgeous view of Sapphire Lake glistening beyond the city drew Jess in as it always had, but this time, she felt no envy. She sat in an oversized armchair across from Camilla's sleek white and gold desk.

Camilla didn't speak, but her laser gaze, the one that had urged many a client into spilling their darkest secrets, cut through Jess's nerves.

Clearing her throat, Jess began, "So, I've been thinking—"

Camilla cut in. "Let me stop you there. I think I know why you're here, Jess. You're not the first to get some time off, meet a guy, and rethink everything you thought you knew. But Jess, you're not just good at this job. You're great at it." Camilla stood and walked to the window, taking in the view Jess guessed she only saw from behind the glass.

She stood silent for an uncomfortable few minutes.

Finally, she spoke again. "Jess, if you decide to leave, I won't try and stop you. We make it our business to know everything about everyone we hire here. And I mean *everything*. People either grow from their past or wither underneath it. The growth you've shown since the day we ushered you in with your wide eyes is nothing short of remarkable." Sitting back down, Camilla faced her once again. "Think long and hard about this, Jess. And if you still want to walk away, I'll do everything I can to make the transition easy for you."

Jess swallowed hard. "I went to see my father again." She took a deep breath. "He still couldn't speak, but he was awake, and I told him all the things I've been needing to say for years. Things I should have said a long time ago. About never feeling settled, never feeling whole. I haven't felt completely safe since I was thirteen, and I've been trying to find my place in this world ever since."

"And you think you've found it now? Outside these four walls?" Camilla gestured to the lake sparkling in the distance.

"Yes," Jess said quietly. "I do."

Camilla came around to Jess and laid a motherly hand on her shoulder. "I would never begrudge you your happiness, Jess. But you still have some time. Think about it a little longer, and then you let me know."

Despite Camilla's uncertainty, when Jess walked out of *Jantzen & Jennings*, she knew in her heart of hearts she was saying goodbye.

CHAPTER NINE

"FIVE MORE DAYS UNTIL CHRISTMAS!" Halle called as Jess rolled in a large suitcase full of barely worn pantsuits. "That's your third load this week, girl!" Halle pranced over to Jess, her eyes bright with anticipation. "Let's see!" Clapping, she unzipped the suitcase before Jess could even register the words.

Jess beamed as Halle exclaimed over each piece. "Jess, this stuff is lit!" Grabbing a bright pink blazer Jess hadn't hesitated to part with, Halle gasped. She rubbed the soft fabric against her cheek. Swooning, she pleaded, "I'll never ask you for anything ever again!"

Jess giggled. "That's what you said yesterday about the lime green pumps!" She shook her head. "Go ahead. Pink's not my color anyway."

A deep voice from behind Jess said, "I disagree. I think you're gorgeous in any color."

Jess blushed, her heartbeat quickening at Cole's compliment.

"More clothes? Do you have anything left to wear, Jess?" His tone was teasing, but his smile shone with approval. "I'm proud of you." He put his arm around her waist and leaned down to kiss the top of her head.

Winking at Jess, Halle disappeared into the back with Jess's clothes, presumably to iron and hang them.

Cole held Jess at arm's length, his hands resting on her shoulders. "Jess, you've done enough. I appreciate all you're doing, but you need to take care of yourself, too."

Leaning her cheek against his rough, warm hand, Jess sighed. "I want to do more. Camilla was right to begin with. I was becoming the job, and I don't want that. There's so much more to life. I want to put my past to good use. I feel like I belong here."

Cole raised an eyebrow. "Jess, what are you saying?"

"I think my unpaid sabbatical may turn into my resignation." She ran a hand through her hair, avoiding Cole's gaze. She knew he wasn't the entitled rich guy she'd expected, but would things change between them if she was no longer on track to have a high-powered job? A job worthy of his status? "I've been putting some feelers out. The legal aid clinic in the county is looking for another staff attorney, and they are eager to have me if I want to take the pay cut."

She plowed ahead. "I want to open another warehouse for you in the city. The legal aid clinic is very low pressure, and I will be able to work from home some. That will give me time to find a space, some volunteers, some business partners." Jess tugged at Cole's hand. "Cole, I want to do this."

Rubbing the stubble on his chin, Cole stepped back. "Jess, this is all a little sudden, isn't it? I mean, one day you're flying out to New York to try and be a part of Fashion Week, and the next it all means nothing?"

Jess reached up and trailed a finger along his jaw. "Cole, this is bigger than you. Than us. When I went to see my dad in the hospital, it healed a lot of things for me. I realized on my way home from that awful place that everything I've been doing in this life has been to prove that I'm better than my upbringing. That I'm going to be somebody." She offered a sheepish half-smile. "But it wasn't until I found this place,"

Jess's hands swept the room, "that I realized what I've been missing all along. A calling."

Pulling her close, Cole murmured in her ear, "Jess, I knew the second that you ran into me at Jitterbugs there was something special about you. I was actually planning to call you that day of the race. I couldn't get your gorgeous eyes and feisty spirit out of my head." He brushed her ear with his lips. "Jess, will you spend Christmas with me?"

Nodding against his chin, Jess tilted her head up until her lips met his. Their kiss was soft and sweet, but when she pulled away, she saw the desire in Cole's eyes.

Leaning in again, her heart pounded against her chest. Their next kiss left her breathless, and Cole stumbled into a table when Halle walked into the room.

"I didn't see nothing, Boss Man," Halle blurted. She cackled and gave them both a thumbs up. "See you both on Christmas Day, then." Halle winked slyly and danced from the room.

"The Twelve Days of Christmas" echoed overhead, but this time, Jess didn't mind one bit.

EPILOGUE

ONE YEAR LATER

"Do you, Jessica Lynn Justice, take this man to be your lawfully wedded husband?" The officiant tried to ignore Hazel chewing on his shoelaces.

"I do," Jess said, hoping her tone conveyed the commitment behind the words.

"And do you, Cole Nicholas Coffman, take this woman to be your lawfully wedded wife?" Hazel moved to gnawing on the officiant's ankle.

"I do." Cole's solemn promise left no doubt in Jess's mind.

The crowd cheered a few moments later as they shared their first kiss as man and wife. Hazel and Annie, emboldened by the noise, barked and pranced around their new family, eager to share in the joy.

*C*ole gazed down at Jess as they twirled around the dance floor, tenderness in his eyes. "Do you remember where we spent last Christmas? The day you fell head over heels?"

Jess laughed. "I had no clue what to expect! The party you threw for all your past and present volunteers really bowled me over. Their obvious respect for you cemented my feelings. I knew you were the one that night."

"It took you that long?" Cole teased. "Watching you at that party interacting with everyone important to me... the way you fit in and had them eating out of the palm of your hand... it was magical." His hands moved across her hips. "Speaking of magical, it was so kind of Camilla to buy you this dress. You look incredible."

"Quite a going-away present," Jess agreed. "I'm so grateful that she's offered to partner with our new location of Fashion Forward. I already have enough inventory to open after the new year. I forgot to tell you in the whirlwind of today that a judge friend of hers has added us to the list of places where teens can earn their community service hours."

Executing another perfect spin, Jess caught her dad's eye and winked. He gave her a warm smile as a tear rolled down his cheek. She leaned against Cole, gratefulness over-whelming her.

Halle came running onto the dance floor, and they both stopped mid-step. "That crazy devil dog got into the cake! I'm so sorry. I turned my back for one second, and the next thing I knew, she was going to town on the icing. I put her in the back of your car for now."

Cole looked at Jess, his eyes wide. "The cake—"

"The car!" Jess reached down to remove her heels.

Fingers still intertwined, they ran off the dance floor together.

Cole gripped Jess's hand as they hurried to the car, Annie trailing behind them. Hazel peeped out the window at them, her doggy grin unable to distract them from the piece of headrest hanging from her mouth. Jess and Cole collapsed in a fit of laughter.

"Our life together might not always be pretty, but I can promise that it will always be interesting," Cole said.

"Want to up the 'interesting' ante?" Jess asked, her tone mysterious.

"What'd you have in mind?"

"Let's just go. Hop in the car with Hazel and Annie and leave. Right now. No cake, no lame speeches, no sparklers. I've had all the photographs I can stand for one night. Let's keep everyone guessing." Jess batted her eyelashes without shame.

"You don't have to ask me twice!" Cole helped Jess shove her ballgown into his car, then hopped into the driver's seat. If the limousine driver noticed his charges making an escape, he stayed silent.

"Let's go, husband." Jess rested her curls against the partially eaten headrest and sighed in contentment.

Cole leaned over and kissed her cheek. "Husband. My new favorite word."

Christmas lights twinkled from the roofs of houses they passed, the reds, greens, and whites giving them an equally beautiful send-off to the fireworks they'd skipped.

The car's tires crunched over the winding gravel driveway, then rolled to a stop just beyond a copse of trees.

Cole announced, "Girls, we're here."

Jess blinked her sleepy eyes as she took in the surroundings. The soft white façade of their new Colonial stood out against the darkness. Jess squeezed Cole's hand as she breathed in the word that she'd been scared of for so long. "Home. I'm finally home."

THE END

MERRY CHRISTMAS, EVELYN

BY AMANDA JEMMETT

CHAPTER ONE

"IT'S OKAY, I understand. I'll stop by for my things tomorrow. Thanks, Whit." I sigh and hang up with my now former boss. I've worked at Whitney's Book Boutique for almost five years. Sales had been slow the last year or so but I never thought she'd go out of business. "This is what happens when people trade their hard copies for e-readers," I mutter to the dogs, clipping on Dixie's leash. That bookstore was by far my favourite place to work, walking these adorable pups a close second.

I step out onto the porch, making sure to lock Mr. Henderson's door behind me and pull up my hood with my free hand. The clouds are dark and dreary but I'm hoping it won't snow until after our walk.

Every Wednesday afternoon is the same—warm up with a quick jaunt to the end of the street, and then break into a jog for the other three kilometers. Once we reach the corner, I continue down the path but don't speed up. After that phone call, I can't get into my groove.

Whitney's store wasn't only my favourite job, it was also my best paying one. I'd hoped to use the small Christmas bonus she gave out each year to spoil my niece since I barely get to see her, but now I have to worry about being able to pay my share of the rent.

Caught up in my thoughts, I don't notice Max coming across a stray feline until the Australian shepherd and his three friends take off at a run, dragging me behind. I yell for them to heel but they ignore my commands and chase the cat further down the street.

I swerve around pedestrians as best I can, tugging on the leashes with all my might, but when working together, these dogs are ridiculously strong. I slip on some black ice and fall forward, losing the leashes and land face first onto the concrete.

"Shit!" I scramble back to my feet, not taking the time to check out my injuries, and chase after the pack. "Max! Beau! Dixie! Lola!" None of the dogs pay attention. I catch up to them when they surround a tree, standing on their hind legs and barking at the cat sitting on a large branch, licking a paw as if nothing had disturbed his morning stroll.

"I think these belong to you," a deep voice says.

I look away from the smug feline to a man, about six foot tall, gripping the leashes in his broad tanned hand.

My gaze strays over fitted blue jeans, past a poufy red coat up to a chiseled jaw and panty-dropping dimples. A scruffy beard covers full lips tilted up in a crooked smile. His bright hazel eyes draw me in. Dark brown, almost black, hair falls into those eyes and I have to stop myself from brushing it off his face.

"Th-thanks," I stutter, finally accepting the leashes and tugging the dogs back to my side.

"You got banged up pretty good," he comments, eyeing my arms.

I look down and see a thin trail of blood coming from my right elbow. "Hazards of the job," I say with a shrug, trying not to show how much it hurt.

"I have a first aid kit at my place, it's only a block away if you want to get those scrapes cleaned up." He hooks a thumb over his shoulder with a sheepish smile.

I laugh. "I'm sorry, and you are...?"

"Name's Caleb." He offers that broad hand and it engulfs mine as we shake.

"Evelyn."

"Well, Evelyn, can I help with your injuries?"

I look over at the dogs wagging their tails with pent up energy. "I appreciate the offer, but I should get back to our walk."

"Is that what you were doing? Looked more like the hundred-yard-dash." He chuckles. "Maybe we could grab a coffee when you're done?"

Butterflies fill my belly as I consider his invitation. I have nothing else to do once I drop off the pups, other than bandaging myself up and I could use some warming up. "I'll be out for another half hour or so but why not?"

Caleb looks at his watch. "Let's meet at Lava Java in an hour?"

Lola whimpers and I scratch her behind the ear. "See you then." With a wave, I continue down the path, fighting the urge to look over my shoulder to see if he's still there.

I hit my head when I fell, so I wouldn't be surprised if I hallucinated the encounter.

CHAPTER TWO

I FINISH BANDAGING up my knee and wriggle into a pair of jeans. I love those dogs, but they're little demons disguised as cuddly angels. Checking my watch, I see that I have fifteen minutes before I need to leave for the café, which is only a five-minute walk. Rather than sit around checking the time every two seconds, I grab my purse and dally over.

The closer I get to the café, the stronger the scent of coffee becomes. I grab the handle but don't open the door when I spot Caleb sitting at a table with a tall, stick thin, and gorgeous, brunette woman. She tucks a stray lock of hair behind his ear as they talk, huddled together.

Not wanting to intrude on their moment, I turn around and quickly walk back the way I came. I'd say men are dogs, but that'd be an insult to canines everywhere.

I wake up early the next day, my chest tight as I shower and dress. I keep hoping Whitney will call saying she doesn't have to shut down her store, but the more time passes, the harder it is to hold on to that thought.

Around noon I give up that hope altogether and slip on my boots. I can't put off cleaning out my locker any longer.

The sun reflects off the snow outside and I groan, shielding my eyes. *This is not the cheery day it appears to be.*

The beauty of living in an apartment in downtown Toronto is that everything you need is within walking distance. It takes only a few minutes to get to Whitney's store and when I step inside the building seems deserted. The lights are dim with no people in sight. If it weren't for Celine Dion playing in the background, I'd wonder if Whit was even here. Given her choice of music, I'd say we're both mourning the loss of this store.

Walking up the aisle to the stockroom slash employee lounge, I scan the bookshelves, disappointed to not see a single customer. I push open the back door and see Whit sitting on a flipped over crate, flask in hand.

"Evvlleeyynnnn," she slurs with a smile when she sees me.

"Hey, girl." I walk over to her and hug her tight.

"Want some?" Whitney extends the flask but I wave it away with a gracious smile.

"I think you've had plenty for the both of us."

She giggles, taking a sip. "You're probably right. It's empty now anyway."

My brows draw together as concern for my friend sets in. I've seen her drink when we get together outside of work, but never this early in the day. "How long have you been sitting here? I think we should get you home." I wrap my arm around her shoulders, and lift her up.

"This is my home! But those bastards are taking it away from me."

"Who's taking the store, sweetie?"

"Those assholes at the bank, won't give me any more time to catch up on my payments."

This is news to me. Yesterday she'd made it sound like she made the decision to close. "I'm sure they're just doing their job, it's not personal."

"Yeah? Feels pretty fucking personal to me. I bet they

enjoy ripping people's dreams to shreds!" Whitney leans against me, her blue tipped bangs fall into her caramel brown eyes and I have to balance the weight before we fall on our asses.

"It's a nice day, why don't we get you some fresh air," I suggest. The alcohol on her breath is making me nauseous.

Whitney follows beside me until we step out onto the sales floor.

"No. If I leave, they'll shut me down sooner. They'll have to drag me out before I give up my store!" She sits on the floor, crossing her arms and legs with a huff of defiance.

Remembering I came here to clean out my locker, I say, "How 'bout I get my things and take you to lunch? You need something other than alcohol in your system."

Whitney sits there, ignoring me. With a sigh, I go back to the stock room and open my locker. The collection of books, pens, and adult colouring sheets beneath my work smock brings the grief flooding back. I grab an empty cardboard box from beside the recycling bin and throw my things into it, too upset to care about packing it all up neatly.

When I make my way out from the back room, Whitney's nowhere to be found. "Shit," I mutter, walking up to where the row of registers are set up. The light in the Manager's Office is on and I breathe a sigh of relief. Placing the box down on a nearby table, I open the door and find Whitney passed out at her desk, cuddling the flask like it's her favourite stuffed teddy bear. She keeps a blanket on top of a filing cabinet for when she's here late at night. I grab it and fold it around her, turning off the light on my way out.

Not willing to take the risk that people will come in while she's asleep, I lock up the store and trudge back to my place. I'm almost at the apartment when I hear my name called behind me. I turn around and see Caleb, waving his arms over his head like a wild man. *Just what I need.*

"Hey," he says, slightly out of breath.

"Hi." I shift the weight of my box, wishing I'd ignored the shouts and gone inside.

"Missed you yesterday. How're the injuries?"

"Good thing you had that brunette to keep you company." I roll my eyes, not in the mood to be the bigger person and swipe my key card, opening the apartment's outer door. Caleb grabs the frame, a frown on his pretty-boy face.

"You saw that, huh?"

"It was hard to miss."

"And if I told you my ex saw me sitting in the coffee shop and came in to talk, would you believe me?"

I pretend to mull it over, but really I wonder why he cares what I think. "Probably not." I shift the box to my other arm.

"Can I convince you to let me explain? I'll even carry your stuff wherever you're going."

I agree and hand it over to him. Once I get to my door I'll take it back and close him out. He follows me to the row of elevators. The ride up the two floors to my apartment is quiet and awkward. The weight of his stare has me struggling to keep my own eyes forward.

When we reach the fifth floor, Caleb follows me down the hall. I get to my door and remove my keychain from my purse. Sliding it into the lock, I turn and reach for the box. But Caleb tucks it against his side.

"Don't worry, I've got it." His lips curl into a knowing smirk and I realize my plan may not be as simple as I'd originally thought. It didn't account for his stubbornness.

Sighing, I open the door and sweep my arm inside, inviting him in. "Fine. You can put it on the kitchen table."

"Yes, ma'am." He steps inside, his eyes scanning over the spacious apartment and landing on a pair of boxers hanging off the back of the couch.

My face heats up and I go to snatch the offending underwear, throwing them into Tyler's room and closing the door. "Sorry, my roommates can be slobs sometimes."

Caleb sets the box on the table and turns to face me.

"None of my business," he says with a shrug, leaning against the table with his arms folded over his buff chest.

Unable to stand still with him watching me, I grab the kettle and fill it with water before setting it on the stove, keeping my back to him. *Some tea will soothe away my nerves.*

"So about yesterday…" he begins.

"Yesterday?" I parrot. "None of my business."

"I think it is." His breath hits my cheek and I close my eyes, trying to focus on breathing evenly.

"If you came to tell me you're getting back together with your 'ex,' don't bother. You don't owe me anything."

He turns me around until I face him, and I'm lost in shimmering jade green eyes.

"And if I came here to tell you that's what she wanted but I turned her down, what would you say then?"

I swallow hard and shrug, feigning disinterest. Looking away at the chipped tile flooring, I ask, "What do you want me to say? Congratulations?"

"You're a stubborn little thing."

Being that I'm only five foot five, he's not wrong. I flash a dazzling smile. "I've been called worse."

The kettle whistles and I turn my back on him again, grabbing a mug from the cupboard and pulling out an Earl Grey tea bag. While I don't want to offer the invitation, I can't break from my upbringing and turn back to Caleb. "Would you like a cup of tea?"

I don't know if he can see that I don't want him here and is messing with me, or if he thinks he's won, but he settles into a seat at the table, his hands resting behind his head, legs crossed at the ankles. "I'd love one."

I set the cup I just poured in front of him, with more force than necessary, tea spilling over the rim.

"Could I get some milk and sugar?" He bats his eyelashes and that's when I know he's toying with me.

I place the carton of milk and bowl of sugar beside his cup before pouring my own and taking a long sip, burning my tongue. We sit in silence, sipping our drinks. I look around the apartment, not willing to meet his eyes or look in his general direction.

"Well, this isn't a café but I'd count this as a re-do first date. Wouldn't you?"

My mouth hangs open and I laugh derisively. "No, I would not."

He leans his elbow on the table, a curious expression in his eyes. "What would you consider a date then?"

"Hmm, I don't know. Corny stuff. Like dinner and a movie, skating under the stars, even mini putt, or billiards."

"Really? I would never have taken you for a mini putt kind of gal."

"And what kind of *gal* do you think I am?" I watch with glee as his own face turns pink before he straightens in his chair, studying me.

"A *woman* who likes getting her hands dirty, but is unique enough to not enjoy conforming to expectations."

He got all that from one interaction? Damn. Would it really be so bad to give him the benefit of the doubt? I've been burned before, but I'd also never met a man as insightful as Caleb.

I swallow the last of my tea, going back and forth on whether to trust him. But I did let him into the apartment... My gut wins out over my head. It's only a date, not a lifetime of commitment.

"So, let's say I believed your little story. How would you make it up to me?"

His eyes twinkle as he smiles a megawatt smile. "What're you doing tonight?"

"I would say nothing, but I have a feeling that's about to change."

"Meet me at seven at Greenwood Park." Standing, Caleb puts his mug in the sink and heads to the door. "Not that it could ever compare to the green of your eyes."

And with that, he's gone.

CHAPTER THREE

I'VE NEVER BEEN to Greenwood Park before, so the walk takes longer than it should. When I finally reach my destination, I can't help but laugh. In front of me are crowds of people milling around in skates waiting for the Zamboni to finish cleaning the outdoor ice rink.

I scan the nearby faces but don't see Caleb anywhere. My heart beats faster, wondering if I'd been duped when arms circle around my waist and my body tingles with electricity.

"You're here," he whispers in my ear.

Caleb turns me around until I face him and his boyish grin.

"You thought I'd stand you up?"

He shrugs. "It may have crossed my mind." He takes my hand and leads me toward a small booth. "What size do you wear?"

"Excuse me?"

"Your skate size."

"Oh, a six please."

Caleb turns to the woman in the booth and hands over a folded bill. "Men's ten and lady's six, please."

The woman turns pale white, a silly grin spreading across her face. "S-Sure. And can I just say, I'm a huge fan." She turns around and pulls the skates from their cubbies and hands them to Caleb who takes them with a strained smile.

A huge fan? What of?

Letting Caleb lead me to an unoccupied bench, I put on my skates but can't help myself when I tease, "She seemed pretty surprised to see you. What're you, famous or something?"

"Or something," he responds with a wink.

I stand up, testing my balance. It's been years since I'd been on the ice.

Caleb grasps my hand. "Ready?"

I nod. We step onto the ice and take it slow. My legs shake beneath me and I struggle to stay upright.

"For someone who says they enjoy skating under the stars, you don't seem very good at it."

"Hey, now. It's been a while, I'm a little rusty." I give him a light nudge with my elbow.

"Careful, missy. You don't want to dish out what you can't take."

Spurred on by his taunt, I nudge him again and try to skate away but he tightens the hold on my hand, quickening his pace and maneuvering around the other patrons until I'm struggling to keep up.

Unwilling to let him win that easy, I try to keep pace but it's not long before my lungs start to burn and I struggle to suck in air.

"Okay, okay. You win," I wheeze. Planting my hands on my knees, I let myself glide.

Caleb skates in circles around me, doing a little dance. I go to step off the ice and trip over Caleb's skate. Unable to keep our balance, we tumble into a snowbank, our limbs tangled. I laugh, trying to catch my breath and struggle to wipe the hair out of my face with my gloves.

Gentle fingers brush my light brown hair away before they reach down and cup my cheeks. My heart races when I look up. Caleb gazes into my eyes as he leans toward me. I hold my breath as his lips sweep over mine in a ghost of a kiss. Wrapping my arms around his neck, I pull him closer and seal my lips over his.

Caleb moves his hands into my hair and I moan against his lips before breaking away, my breathing no more in control now than it was on the ice.

"Wow," I whisper to myself.

"My thoughts exactly."

I blush, not meaning to have said that aloud.

Taking my hand, Caleb helps me out of the snow. "Hot chocolate?"

A shiver runs through me, frozen from head to toe. "That would be great."

"We should probably get it to go. No offense, but you look like a human popsicle."

I laugh. "None taken, I feel like one, too."

"Can I take you back to my place? I can throw your wet things in the dryer. It's only a two-minute walk from here."

I debate the twenty-minute hike it'd take me to get to my apartment, but my body shakes violently from the cold.

"This isn't a move. I promise," he says earnestly.

"O-O-Ok-kay." I wrap my arms around me, falling onto the bench. My fingers are numb and it becomes impossible to untie my laces.

Caleb kneels in the snow, resting my foot in his lap. He helps remove my skates and even slides on my boots.

"On second thought, I have hot chocolate in the pantry." He removes his own skates with lightning speed, wrapping me in his arms and rubbing his palms along my back. The cold fades for a moment, but the second he lets go, I'm shivering again.

We return our skates to the booth and I follow Caleb, telling myself it's only a drink, nothing is going to happen, that he's being a gentleman by not letting me freeze to death. Okay, so the last one's a bit of an exaggeration, but still, *nothing is going to happen.*

"Do you always walk so many dogs at once?" Caleb asks out of the blue.

"Yep. Every Wednesday. I could walk them on different days but I don't have the heart to separate them."

"What kind of dogs are they?"

"Well, you've got Max, the Australian shepherd. Lola, a little Dalmatian puppy. Dixie, who's a Boykin spaniel, and Beau, a border collie pup."

"I'm impressed."

I can't help laughing. "Let me guess, because you don't think a girl like me is strong enough to manage?"

He stops and faces me. "Not everything is an insult to your womanly capabilities, you know."

Do I know that, though? "Whatever you say."

"Do you have a favourite?"

"Favourite dog? No. Dixie is by far the calmest and easiest to walk, but I love watching Beau's floppy little ears when he runs. They're almost too big for his face!"

We continue walking a few minutes more before Caleb stops at a mansion-sized house. "Big place for one guy," I comment as casually as possible.

"Thanks. I've been told I could fit a whole hockey team in here."

He walks up to the gate and keys in a code. The doors slowly swing open and he takes my hand once more. I follow him up on autopilot, gawking at the winter wonderland that is his lawn. *Family home? Is he an actor or something?* Christmas figurines and ice sculptures are everywhere. The only clear space is the driveway and cobblestoned path to the door. Bright lights cover the roof while Christmas music quietly plays from a hidden speaker.

"Is it safe to assume Christmas is your favourite holiday?"

"What can I say? I'm a sucker for the carols."

As Caleb opens the large double doors, the first thing I see is brightly polished marble. The cream and gold veined stone covers the floor and walls. The stairs, a dark mahogany lending warmth to the otherwise cold space, sweep up to either side of the front hall. Both sides of the foyer open into even grander rooms, the dining area to the right, and the simple but elegant living room to the left.

"Holy shit," I breathe, staring up at the grand chandelier.

Gripping my hand, Caleb leads me through the living room, down another hallway, toward the back of the house. He opens the door and flicks on a switch.

"Bottom one's the dryer. I'll go get you some dry clothes," he says before closing the door.

I look around the spacious laundry room and begin undressing. *What does he do to be able to afford all this? The lady at the rink said she was a big fan, but of what?* A knock at the door interrupts my thoughts and I go to open it a crack. I grab black sweatpants and a light blue t-shirt with a laugh and close the door. Changing into the borrowed, baggy attire, I pull the drawstring of the sweats as tight as they'll go.

Throwing my wet clothes in the dryer, I set it to quick dry and walk out, smack into Caleb's chest. His arms wrap around to keep me steady. We stand there, staring into each other's eyes and I'm speechless.

His mouth descends on mine and I weave my fingers in his luscious brown locks. His hands move to the back of my thighs and he lifts me up with ease. I cross my legs around his waist and let him carry me away.

CHAPTER FOUR

LATER THAT NIGHT, I stare up at the ceiling of Caleb's room, my unanswered questions at the front of my mind. Why should it bother me that he hasn't told me what he does for a living? I haven't either. Hell, we don't even know each other's last names.

I slip out of his arms and slide on the oversized t-shirt before tiptoeing out of the room and down the spiraling flight of stairs, searching for the kitchen. I go right when I reach the foyer but end up back in the same hallway with the laundry room. Retracing my steps, I head toward the dining area and follow the path to a gourmet style kitchen the size of my apartment. I open cupboard after cupboard, searching for a glass before giving up and digging around the fridge for a bottle of water, dehydrated after our little... excursion.

I meander through the halls, gazing up at beautiful artwork hanging from the walls and what I can only assume are family photos decorating small tables. *Such a large house for one man.* The little voice in the back of my head tells me to snoop for the answers I seek, but it feels like a betrayal of Caleb's trust when he welcomed me into his home. Instead, I walk back upstairs, slip under the covers, and nuzzle into Caleb's chest, letting sleep and his warmth take me.

$\mathcal{T}$he next morning, I'm startled awake by a high-pitched shriek. I burrow further into the comforter and cover my ears with a pillow.

The blanket flies off my body, leaving me cold. I peek an eye open and find the woman from the café standing at the end of the bed. I scramble to sit up straight, tugging the t-shirt as far down as it will go to cover my mostly naked form.

"Who the *fuck* do you think you are?" she wails, her ice blue eyes wild.

"I... uhh..."

I look over and see Caleb slowly coming to. *How was he sleeping through her shrieking?*

"Savannah?" His voice is deep with sleep but the confusion in his tone is unmistakable.

"Why is *she* in *my* bed?"

My cheeks heat and I look around for the sweatpants I'd worn the night before. I throw them on before shooting Caleb the dirtiest look I can muster. "Lose my number, asshole."

I run out of the room, ignoring his pleas for me to wait. How could I have been such a fool? I should have followed my gut and stayed far away when I saw them at the coffee shop.

I'm halfway down the cobblestone path when I realize I don't know how to open the gate. Spotting an intercom on the side, I press the button. "Open the damn gate."

"If you'd just let me explain—"

"I gave you your chance, now let me out," I yell, cutting him off.

The intercom buzzes and the gates open slowly. I push my way through the second the space is big enough and make the trek back into town.

CHAPTER FIVE

I SPENT the week leading up to Christmas ignoring Caleb's numerous calls and texts while letting Whitney crash at my place until she figures out her next move. I picked up more dog walking shifts to make up for my loss of income with the bookstore and barely scraped enough together to cover my rent.

Whitney has had a bottle in her hand almost every night this week. I can hear her crying when I go to bed and my heart breaks. I keep wishing I had a way to help her, help *us*.

What a lousy and depressing Christmas.

My roommates, Tyler and Kayleigh, had already left for their respective family holidays and the apartment would be all ours for the next two weeks. I'd usually be at my brother's house out in Newfoundland, but I can't afford the travel this year, so I never bothered to pick up a tree of my own.

The door opens and Whitney walks in, stamping the snow off her boots. She sets a large pepperoni and green pepper pizza on the table and we each grab a slice, curling up on the couch to watch a rerun of *Friends*. You can't go wrong with "'The One with the Holiday Armadillo.'"

"Merry Christmas," I sigh, lifting up my slice to toast with hers. "How're you feeling?" I ask, taking a bite of the ooey gooey goodness.

"I'll feel better when I get my store back," she snaps.

I know her anger isn't directed at me, so I give her shoulder a comforting squeeze and focus on the show, wishing again that there was something I could do to help.

We'd just finished the episode when the apartment's buzzer rings. I untangle my legs from Whit's and hold the intercom button. "Yes?"

"Package for a Ms. Evelyn King."

I hit the button beside the intercom, allowing the deliveryman to make his way in. Minutes later, the doorbell rings and I dry my hands on the way to the door, watching Whitney nurse a bottle of vodka. The slim package is wrapped with cartoon Santa heads and snowmen in shimmering silver paper, an envelope taped to the top. I look down the hall, but the deliveryman is nowhere to be found. I kick the door closed, removing the card from the package.

Evelyn,

This is the last time I will try to explain myself, I promise.

I didn't lie when I said Savannah is my ex, but she isn't happy and is refusing to accept the break up. The day you walked out, I found out she had a key to my house made and we got into it. When she finally left, I changed the code to my front gate and all the locks. I told her if she came around again I'd call the police and I haven't seen her since.

Let me make this up to you. Come to 7852 Whittley Rd. If you don't show up by midnight, I understand and you'll never hear from me again.

- Caleb

J stare at the package, mulling Caleb's words over. Should I open it? I'm dying to know what's inside, but how can I when I don't know if I believe him? *It's the same thing he said when he saw me at my apartment, he even went as far as making sure it didn't happen again by changing his code and locks. If he changed them.*

"Evelyn King, have you been holding out on me?" Whitney's voice breaks through and I give my head a small shake. "What's that?"

"Nothing." I stare at the package, debating tossing it away.

"Looks too pretty to be nothing," she remarks behind me.

I fall onto the couch. "I went on a date with this guy, and... stayed the night, which would have been fine if I hadn't woken up half naked to his 'ex' screaming in my face."

"What's with the air quotes?"

I look over at Whitney's sweet, hopeless romantic face. "I'm not sure I believe him."

"Sweetie, not every guy is like Isaac. They aren't all cheating scum." She gives my shoulders a rub.

"I know. It just all seems too convenient."

Whitney plucks the card from my hand, studying it. "Well, if you have questions, why don't you go over and ask him? I can come, give you my two cents if you need it."

Whitney takes the package and tears the wrapping paper open. Inside the long box is a sleeveless, red satin dress with an embroidered bodice and flowing skirt, a pair of black stilettos tucked underneath, both in my size.

I pull them out of the box, inspecting the formal wear. *Does he want me to wear this tonight? Do I have to return them if I don't show?* At least he was smart enough to remove the tags and the evidence of how much he spent on such elegant attire.

I think back to the night on the ice and how marvelous the evening had been. The conversation flowed freely, his touch warmed me, and I haven't been able to stop thinking about him since.

Fuck it. It's not like I have anything better to do on Christmas. "Promise you won't let me get fooled?" I ask, dropping the dress back in the box and turning to Whitney with my patent puppy dog eyes.

"Always, luvvie."

"Guess we'd better get ready." I stand up and carry the box into my room, tossing it on my bed before going into the bathroom and taking a long hot shower, scrubbing and shaving every inch of skin I can reach.

I blow dry my hair and twist it up into the only up-do I can manage. Making a loose ponytail and parting the middle, I fold the ponytail over. It was a style my mom taught me when I was younger—similar to Belle's look from *Beauty and the Beast* —but when I look in the mirror, I cringe and pull the elastic band from my hair, leaving it to cascade freely down my back.

I paint my nails and toes a bright green in the spirit of the season and when they're finally dry, I put on the gown. The clock on my dresser says it's four-thirty in the afternoon, and the sun is already beginning to set.

I meet Whitney in the kitchen, stunned by the simple beauty of her emerald green, long-sleeved lace panel dress.

Not wanting to walk in such high heels, I call an Uber and we head down to the lobby, my oversized winter coat keeping out the cold every time the building door opens.

The drive is short and I find myself back at Caleb's mansion. This time the gate is open and dozens of cars line the wide roundabout driveway. I thank the driver and climb out, once again stunned by his beautiful home.

"Holy shit. Who is this guy?" Whitney exclaims.

I look over with a nervous smile. "I'm about to find out."

My legs shake as I make my way up the steps and into the now crowded foyer where a maid takes my coat. Men are decked out in tailored suits and tuxedos, the women in long flowy dresses similar to my own.

Further inside, I can hear a band playing acoustic Christmas carols as a young waiter carrying a tray of cham-pagne flutes passes by. I scoop one up, hoping to calm my nerves. My feet move of their own accord and I scan each room, wondering where Caleb is.

Hands cover my eyes. "Boo."

"Santa? Is that you?" I tease, turning around.

The hands leave my sight and I'm face to face with a smiling Caleb wearing a sharp black tux over a crisp white shirt with a red and green polka dot Christmas bowtie.

"You came."

I stare at his scruffy beard, knowing I'll melt away if I look into those mesmerizing eyes. "I almost didn't."

"Holler if you need me," Whitney whispers before disappearing toward the dining room. I'd forgotten she was even here.

Caleb takes my hand, leading me away from the crowds. "I'm glad you did," he says softly.

I fight the shiver his voice elicits and try to steady my racing heart.

"I haven't completely forgiven you yet, I'm still not sure I can trust you."

He leads me into the room from which I'd fled and I sit on the edge of the bed, fiddling with the strap of my clutch.

"What can I say to change your mind?" he asks, closing the door and sitting beside me.

I stare out the large bay window watching the glorious Christmas scene below—crowds of people milling about, smiling and laughing. The wide array of decorations littering the lawn. The kids running between them all in a game of tag —as I consider his question. What could he say? Was there anything that could change my mind? Isn't that why I was here? To forgive him?

I'd already "been there and done that" when it comes to cheaters. They're smooth liars. How do I figure out what the truth is? Or do I walk away now, always wondering "what if?"

I turn back to Caleb. "Let's start with an easy question.

Why was that woman at the rink a big fan? Who are you?" That had seriously been bugging me this whole time.

He chuckles lightly, running a hand through his hair. "I'd guess she's a hockey fan. You may know me by my last name —Brimley. I play for the Toronto Titans. This is actually my year to throw the team Christmas party. That's my team and their families downstairs right now."

"Why didn't you say that when we were out?"

Caleb loses his smile and clears his throat, looking away. "When I tell a girl that, all she sees are dollar signs and celebrity status. I wanted to know that you liked me for me."

"I did. I thought you were funny and kind." I pause. "And *un*attached."

"She really is in my past," he says, turning impassioned eyes on me. Grasping my hands, he rubs his thumbs along the back. "Won't you give me a chance to prove it?"

I study his handsome face. Full lips set in a straight, earnest line, his eyes stare into mine with an emotion I can't quite place. *Would a man really try this hard to convince a woman if he was stepping out? Wouldn't it be much easier to find someone else to fool?*

"Don't make me regret this," I breathe.

His hands drop mine and delve into my hair, his lips kissing my face in a flurry. I laugh under the attack and wrap my arms around his neck, finding his lips with my own.

"Merry Christmas, Evelyn."

THE END

IT FEELS LIKE HOME

BY NIKOLETT STRACHAN

DECEMBER 22

CHARLOTTE

What did I just do? This can't be happening.

"Charlotte? Are you okay?" Sarah's voice sounded far away as she waved a hand in my face, trying to snap me out of my daze.

"Yeah. I'm totally fine." My voice said one thing, but my body felt another.

"How did it go? You don't sound fine." Sarah came out from behind her desk and helped me to the couches in the waiting area of the office. I sat down and let out a giant sigh as relief flushed over me.

"I got it. I got the contract," I finally managed to say.

"What? That's amazing. I knew you would." She gave me a congratulatory hug. "That's why I suggested you for the job. There's no one better."

My best friend's confidence in me should have given me a boost. It was because of her that my little party planning business got the contract to take over the planning of Aurora Heights's annual Holiday Festival. Since starting the business a year ago, I had only ever planned a few birthdays and anniversary parties. Planning the town's biggest celebration of the year was a huge deal for me, and I was way in over my head. With the sudden illness of the original planner, I only had two days to get everything together.

"I don't think I'm going to take the job," I said suddenly. "This is a great opportunity, but two days for the biggest party in Aurora Heights is not enough time."

"Nonsense." Sarah got up and went over to her desk. She pulled out a folder and handed it to me. In it were contracts of all the vendors and a list of things that still needed to be done. "Nora already booked the band and the caterers. All you have to do is set up everything. And find a Santa."

"Okay. That's not so bad." The unease was starting to settle in my chest. There was still a lot to do, but thankfully Nora was organized enough to keep a folder. "How is Nora doing? Have you spoken to her?"

"I spoke to her husband when I went over to her place to pick up the folder for you. Whatever flu she caught has put her out of commission, but her husband said she should be okay."

"I'm glad to hear it. And thank you again for recommending me. This is going to be huge for Pie in the Sky Parties. I just hope I can pull this off."

"Charlotte, you need to relax. If anyone can do it, it's you."

That was easy for her to say. She wasn't the one who had to decorate the entire park in two days. I put the folder into my bag, said goodbye to Sarah, and left city hall. I had decorations to track down and only two days to set everything up. My assistant, Ivy, was wonderful but she was not going to be happy about having to put together a sound system. And I needed a Santa? Great.

I slid into my car and turned up the heat. I blew hot breath into my hands, trying desperately to warm them up. My mind was going a mile a minute. If I could pull this off, Pie in the Sky Parties might actually be profitable. "Okay, Charlotte. You can do this."

SAM

"What's there to do in this town anyway?" I dropped my rucksack on the floor and flopped onto my brother's couch. Nick was on the rucksack like an ant on honey, tucking it neatly into a corner. Heaven forbid I mess up his apartment. Even though he housed a German shepherd named Rex, the place was spotless.

"There's lots to do here, actually," Nick said. "The Holiday Festival is in two days, so that'll be fun."

"Two days? What am I supposed to do until then?"

Rex jumped onto the couch, wagging his tail back and forth as he dropped a red ball into my lap. I took it, ready to throw it for him when Nick yelled, "Not in the house!"

I rolled it across the floor, and he gave me a disappointed look. "Sorry, buddy. Chief's orders." Rex jumped from the couch and reluctantly fetched the ball.

"I know that Aurora Heights is different from the city," Nick began. "But it's not that bad. Once you learn to slow down, it's actually kind of nice."

My big brother used to be a hard-nose detective in Vancouver. He was so uptight that he could break a tree in half just by looking at it. Now, he was still that neat freak, but small-town living seemed to have calmed him down. Maybe that's why my parents insisted I visit him for the holidays this year. Plus, their trip to the Caribbean would have left me alone on Christmas.

"I'm glad you finally took my advice and chilled out, Nicko," I said.

He rolled his eyes as he sat beside me on the couch. "Yeah, okay. I definitely needed to slow down a little. What about you? Have you given your career any thoughts?"

I swallowed the annoyance building in my chest. I knew it. Mom and Dad had sent me here so that big brother Nick could talk some sense into me. I didn't have a career and didn't plan on getting one either. "Careers just tie you down. There's a whole world out there to see."

"But that requires money, which you've been borrowing from Mom and Dad too much."

"Did they put you up to this?"

"No. You know how they are. I'm just looking out for you, Sam. You can't go through life drifting from one person's couch to another."

"I just… don't know what I want to do with my life. I'm not like you. I didn't want to be a cop while I was still in diapers. I'm still trying to figure it all out."

"Don't you think you need to settle down somewhere so you *can* figure things out? Maybe keep a job longer than a week? You're twenty-five now, and it's time to pick something."

I was twenty-six but correcting him would only further prove his point. Besides, that wasn't fair. My last job at the Pick 'n Save warehouse lasted at least a month.

"Are you seriously going to be lecturing me the whole time I'm here?"

"No." He got up and began putting on his wool coat. "I have to get back to the station. But I will find ways to dig at you every now and then, don't worry," he said with a wink and an annoying smirk.

"You wouldn't be my brother if you didn't."

Nick left and then it was just me on the couch with Rex staring at me, waiting for me to make a move. "What are we gonna do, buddy?" Rex's eyes shifted to behind the door where his leash hung. "You want to go for a walk?"

His tail began wagging furiously. He got up and bolted to the door, letting out a few barks before I finally got up and put my coat on. "At least you don't nag me about getting my life together." As soon as I put the leash on him, Rex dragged me out the door.

Aurora Heights was the kind of town you see in those cheesy Christmas movies they play all month long on TV. The shops were all tiny with large, beautifully decorated windows. People walking by stopped to say hi to each other. Some even stopped to say hi to Rex. Even though the air was sharp with cold, no one seemed to mind. No one huddled together and muttered angrily at the falling snow and patches of ice on the ground. I would see why Nick liked this place.

I had no idea where I was going, so I let Rex take me around town. He led me to the center of town to a large park. With snow falling softly on the trees, the place looked like something on a Christmas card.

"This is your stomping grounds?" I asked as Rex waited eagerly for me to take off his leash so I could throw his ball. "Okay, okay. Sit."

He sat and I took off the leash. He leaped at the red ball in my hands, eager to go chase after the thing. I threw it as hard as I could and he bolted after it, kicking snow up in his wake.

I couldn't help but laugh. Sometimes, I wished that I was a dog. I wished that all I had to worry about was eating, sleeping, and chasing after a ball. But I knew that Nick was right. Eventually, I was going to have to settle down. But why worry about that while on Christmas vacation?

Rex happily ran back to me with the red ball in his mouth and dropped it in front of me for another throw. I walked a few feet toward the street and threw the ball... and cringed. The ball, along with Rex, was headed straight for a woman carrying a very large box of what looked like Christmas decorations. The ball hit the box as Rex jumped on the woman, knocking her into the snow. The box flew into the air, sending Christmas tree ornaments flying and breaking as they landed on the shoveled pavement.

"No!" I ran toward the dog, who was busy sniffing the woman in the snow. "I'm so sorry. Are you okay?"

When she managed to brush blonde hair from her face, I was met with the most beautiful hazel eyes I'd ever seen. My stomach felt weak, especially as the woman frowned. That was the cutest frown I'd ever seen on a face.

"This is not a smiling matter," she said to me. I hadn't realized that I was smiling. "Rex, how could you?"

"You know Rex?"

She moved to pet the dog, who gave her a lick as if to say sorry and ran off to find his ball. "Of course I know Rex. Everyone in town does."

I reached out a hand to help her up. "Rex just got a little excited." My face burned as I talked to the woman. Did it just get warmer out here?

"Yes, well, he should be on a leash." She brushed snow out of her hair and off her coat, then surveyed the damages. "Oh no. No, no, no. They're all broken. What am I going to do?"

"Yeah, sorry about that."

"Sorry? These were the decorations for the Holiday Festival."

"Again, I'm really sorry," I said. I was not making a good first impression on this woman.

"Well, sorry isn't good enough. I'm calling the police."

"The police? What for?"

"For... for... ruining the Holiday Festival."

She pulled her phone out of her pocket and dialed. She was serious. She was actually calling the police over this. Aurora Heights seemed like a place that took their Holiday Festival very seriously, so I had no doubt that I was going to be in big trouble.

CHARLOTTE

"I understand that the festival is in two days, but I can't just arrest Sam." Nick DeLuca stood with his hands on his hips, looking like an older version of the man who had single-handedly ruined the Holiday Festival.

"It's because he's your brother, isn't it?" I crossed my arms over my chest, letting him know that I wasn't having any of his nepotism. Nick was a good detective, but even he had his faults.

"It's not that. Believe me if I could arrest him for something, I would." He shot his brother a look that made Sam open his mouth in protest. Luckily, he knew where the line was and didn't say anything. "But ruining the Holiday Festival isn't an arrestable offense."

"What about Rex? He should've been on a leash." I pointed at the dog beside Nick, who lowered his head. A pang in my stomach made me feel bad so I gave him a pat on the head.

"Yes, Rex should've been on a leash, and Sam's getting a ticket for that."

"A ticket? That's it? He ruined my decorations! I have two days until the festival and now I have no decorations!"

"I don't know what to tell you," Nick said with a sympathetic shrug.

"I do." A familiar voice came from behind me. It was Lainey Boggins, the reporter for the Aurora Heights Chronicle. She was doing a story about me taking over for Nora this year and had set up to do an interview. And now here she was, witnessing what a disaster I was already. Still, she turned to me and smiled. "I think I have a solution to your problems."

"Really?"

"Seriously?" Nick asked.

"Yeah. Sam can work off the damages by helping you as a volunteer."

It took a few moments for her words to sink in. She wasn't serious. "You can't be serious."

"Why not? Sam's only in town for a few days, and I know you could use the help setting up," Nick said.

Darn. They had a point. I really, *really* needed the help. I let out a frustrated sigh before I said, "Fine."

"Great. It's settled. No arrest for Sam and you get help. And we can reschedule the interview if you'd like."

"Yes, that would be ideal."

Lainey looked pretty pleased with herself as she exchanged a look with Nick. He gave her a knowing smile... and was that a wink? "Now, Nick. I need to talk to you about the case—"

"Of course you do," he groaned. I couldn't help but laugh. Everyone in town loved how they bantered. Some even had a pool going on when they would end up together. "Are we all good here?" Nick asked.

"Yes," I said reluctantly.

"No," Sam said. "Isn't anyone going to ask what I want here?"

"Sam, you ruined Charlotte's decorations. The least you can do is help set up for the festival," Nick said. "Besides, it'll keep you out of trouble."

"Technically, it was Rex who ruined—" Nick gave him a glare that made Sam stop arguing. "Fine," he huffed.

I picked up the box and began cleaning up the broken ornaments. I had taken every single Christmas decoration from my apartment for this, and now they were all ruined. I was going to have a heck of a time trying to find more.

"Guess it's just you and me," Sam said with a smile, which I'm sure charmed the pants off every woman he met.

"Just help me clean up," I shot at him. If he thought that I was going to fall for his charm and good looks, he was going to have a rude awakening. I'd known men like him. My ex-boyfriend was just like him: good-looking with nice hair and a charming smile. But underneath his charm was a selfish, overgrown child, and I had no doubt that Sam DeLuca was no different.

"I know I've already said this, but I'm really, *really* sorry about this mess," Sam said after we'd cleaned up the broken ornaments.

"Yes, well, you can make it up to me by finding decorations and meeting me here with them tomorrow morning. Seven o'clock. Sharp."

"Seven o'clock... in the morning?" His big, soft brown eyes turned to dinner plates. If he was anyone else, I might have thought he looked adorable.

"Yes, in the morning. Just because you're on holiday doesn't mean you can mess this up for me. This is a big deal so please be on time."

I had a feeling that he wasn't going to be on time.

DECEMBER 23

SAM

I DIDN'T CARE how cute Charlotte was. I didn't care how gorgeous her eyes were or how much I liked the way her blonde hair glistened in the sun. She was too… what was the word? Organized? Tightly wound? Definitely tightly wound. She needed to relax. It was Christmas, after all. Maybe that's what it was. Maybe she was one of those people that Christmas brought out their inner stress monkey. Growing up, my mom was like that. Everything had to be perfect, everything had to be pristine and clean. It stressed me out just being around her.

Which is why I vowed to always take it easy, to always be chill. Nothing was ever worth getting so worked up over. Especially Christmas.

I'd stayed up late looking for Christmas decorations in Nick's place. He'd put out a small plastic tree without any decorations on a side table in his living room. He'd said he was too busy working to decorate, so I put every decoration I could find in the apartment into a box and hauled it over to the park the next morning. I didn't exactly tell Nick, but I was sure he wouldn't mind. The decorations were minimal and mostly consisted of various lights, but after yesterday, I had to put in some effort. Which is more than I normally do, so it was saying a lot. But I wanted to do this. I wanted to prove to my brother that I wasn't aimless, that I could do some real work if I wanted to.

"You showed up on time." Charlotte looked surprised when I found her unpacking boxes at her car "And you got decorations."

"I can't believe you doubted me." I flashed her my best smile, but she repaid me with a frown.

"Yes, well, thank you for doing the bare minimum. Follow me."

This woman was ridiculous. She was like every teacher in school I'd ever had. Except none of them were this good looking. I shook the thought out of my head. Nothing could happen between us, even if she wasn't so… commanding. I was only here for a few days, and I wanted to make the most of my time here. One organized, stickler-for-the-rules kind of person was enough to deal with.

We made our way to a gazebo in the middle of the park. "Okay, I need help setting up the sound system for the band. Then we have to hang the decorations. I was thinking lights around the gazebo. Then tables for catering over there." She pointed to a place that was stacked with plastic tables. "Vendors are going to be over there, but most of them have their own stuff—"

"Okay, okay, one thing at a time," I said. My head was already spinning.

Charlotte let out a frustrated sigh. "Sound system first. Do you think you can handle that? I have to check on my assistant. She should've been here by now."

"Sound system. Got it." I looked at the mass of speakers and wires in the middle of the gazebo. I'd never set up a sound system before, but how hard could it be? I place the box of decorations down and went over to the pile. I pulled out wires upon wires and plugs and things that looked like it belonged in an alien spaceship. I found my phone and searched "how to set up a sound system."

CHARLOTTE

I didn't expect him to show up at all, let alone on time. With a box of decorations. Most of them were too small to really be seen anywhere, but the lights were going to come in handy. After yesterday's debacle, I had to rethink the entire decor. Lights were easy to put up and always looked good. I wished I had more time to come up with a color scheme, but my assistant, Ivy, said that we barely had enough time to track down enough lights let alone do something elaborate. She was right.

I left Sam in the gazebo to deal with the sound system, but when I saw him pull out his phone, a pang of anxiety hit my chest. He'd better be researching how to put that sound system together. I couldn't afford dead weight on my team.

"Deal with it in a minute, Charlotte." I let out a long and slow exhale, trying to calm my nerves. Where was Ivy? She was supposed to be here by now. I pulled out my phone to give her a call when I saw her making her way through the snow with her kids toddling behind her and throwing snow at each other.

"I'm sorry I'm late," she said. "The babysitter called in sick. Said she caught that nasty flu going around. I had no choice but to bring these two."

I looked at her twins, Theo and Maddy, who looked back at me with large eyes, red cheeks, and snotty noses. They were too adorable to send away. Besides, at ten years old, they might be able to help with some lighter work.

"It's okay. They can help," I said.

"Thanks, Charlotte. I owe you," Ivy said. She grabbed a table for catering and began setting up.

"It's okay. These things happen," I said. The kids began

153

running around, throwing themselves on the ground and making snow angels. "Besides, they're good kids."

"They are not, and you know that," Ivy said with a laugh.

I began helping her with the tables when I felt something cold and wet hit the back of my head. I turned to find Theo and Maddy giggling as they bent over to form more snowballs.

"Hey, kids!" Sam waved at them from the gazebo. "You wanna play a game?"

They looked at each other, then back at Sam with suspicion. "What kind of game?" Maddy answered.

"Let's see who can untangle wires the fastest."

Ivy leaned over to me and whispered, "That's the guy from yesterday?"

"Yup." I wasn't enthused about his lack of progress with the sound system, but if he was volunteering to keep the kids busy and *not* throwing snowballs at me, I wasn't going to object.

"He's way cuter than you described." Ivy turned to her kids and said, "Go help the nice young man and you can have ice cream later."

"Okay," they said in unison. They ran up to the gazebo and Sam happily put them to work.

"He's pretty good with kids." Ivy looked impressed at Sam's ease with her twins. "Those two don't listen to anyone."

I had to admit that she was right. Then again, Sam seemed like a big kid himself, so I wasn't surprised.

Just like my ex. He was a big kid, too. Selfish and only thought about his own comfort. But he never would have shown up on time or offered to help, let alone entertain children. Maybe I'd misjudged Sam.

"Did you call your uncle about being Santa?" I asked Ivy.

"Yes. He says he'll do it."

"Oh, thank goodness! I thought I was going to have to put the suit on myself." We really needed a Santa, if only because it was tradition. What's a Holiday Festival without a Santa Claus?

"Although Sam looks like he might make a good Santa."

"Sam?" I looked over at the gazebo. He was running around, plugging in giant cords while the kids used his phone as a stopwatch to time him. I couldn't help but smile. "Nah. Too skinny."

"So is my uncle." Ivy gave me a knowing smirk, but I brushed it off. I knew that look. I knew exactly what she was thinking, and it wasn't going to happen. Nothing was going to happen between Sam and me.

*I*t took all day, but the tables were set, the decorations were hung—in odd places, but they were up—and the sound system was finally done. It had taken Sam most of the day to set it up, but he was doing it while entertaining two rowdy kids and I couldn't help but be impressed. All that was left to do was to wrap some lights around the posts and rails of the gazebo. The rest could be done in the morning before the festival. The anxiety that I had been pushing back all day was starting to finally disappear.

The sun was gliding toward the horizon and an icy chill was setting into the already cold air. I shivered. I was tired and I couldn't remember the last time I had eaten. I had sent Ivy home because the kids needed to eat and get ready for bed. After finishing with the sound system, Sam had declared that he was going to find coffee and that was over two hours ago. I wasn't expecting him to come back. He had already exceeded my expectations as far as work ethic went, but I wished he'd come back. I kind of like seeing him... *No Charlotte. Get those thoughts out of your head right now.*

I picked up a string of lights and began wrapping them around the railing.

"Oh good, you're still here," a voice said behind me. Sam made his way up the steps of the gazebo with two large coffees in his hand. He handed one to me, then picked up another string of lights and began wrapping it around a large post. "Sorry I'm late. I got caught up chatting with some people at this café I found. It's a cat café. I've never been to one before." He said it so excitedly that it was difficult not to smile.

"Yeah, that's Dylan Sawyer's café. He has the best coffee in town." I took a sip of the coffee and instantly felt better, warmer. "Thanks for the coffee. And for coming back to help."

"Of course. I'm not going to leave you hanging." He gave me a smile, a genuine smile this time, and I felt a little warmer inside. I really had misjudged him. Sam DeLuca wasn't such a bad guy after all. In fact, he was downright lovable.

SAM

I really liked today. I liked the chill in the air that kept me moving. I liked setting up a sound system with two rowdy ten-year-olds. I liked walking down Aurora Heights's main street and stopping at all the shops. I'd only been in town for a day, and I already had people calling me by name.

But mostly, I liked working with Charlotte. I liked that she didn't get mad at her assistant for bringing her kids to work. I liked that she worked alongside us and didn't just boss us around like I thought she would. She wasn't what I was expecting at all.

"You ever think about moving to the city?" I asked while I wrapped the last of the lights around the gazebo's pole. "You could do really well planning parties there."

"I did think about it. I even had a job offer working with a big event planner, but I turned it down," she said. She let out a wistful sigh. "Sometimes I think about what could've been, but I couldn't take the job. I couldn't leave my home. I love Aurora Heights."

"This place is… different. I can see why Nick likes it here," I said.

She finished with the lights and sat down on the steps of the gazebo beside me. She cradled the coffee in her hands and took a sip. "This place is special. I want to give back to the town that raised me, so I really want this festival to go off without a hitch."

"With your organization skills, it will."

I had been wrong about Charlotte. She wasn't some hard-nosed, bossy woman. She was someone who really cared about people. She cared about this town. She wasn't tightly-wound. She was just stressed out. If I had only two days to plan the biggest festival of the year, I probably would've been stressed out, too.

Luckily, I had the perfect remedy for stress.

I put my coffee cup down and leaped into the snow. I made a small snowball and threw it at her. Not hard, but hard enough for it to explode on her arm.

"What was that for?" she asked indignantly.

"Come on. You need to blow off some steam." I motioned for her to join me in a good old-fashioned snowball fight.

"No, I don't." She sounded like a kid throwing a tantrum and I couldn't help but laugh.

"Yes, you do. Come on." I threw another snowball at her. This time, I caught her right in the face.

"Okay, that's it." She got up and stormed down the steps of the gazebo. The challenge had been accepted.

She made a large snowball and threw it at me, getting me in the chest.

"Is that the best you can do?" I laughed.

"Not even close."

She made another ball of snow and threw it at my face. Then another. The snowballs kept coming as we chased each other around throwing snow like children. When I'd lost strength to make a snowball, I picked up snow and pressed it

157

into her face. She fell into the snow and began howling with laughter. It was the most beautiful sound I'd ever heard.

"You were right," she said as she gasped for air. "I did need that."

We sat in the snow, our faces inches from each other. A force pulled me closer to her, pulled me to her warmth and soft face, making me wonder what her lips tasted like. I leaned in ever so slightly. She did the same. We sat there, inches from touching.

"We should get going," she said, breaking whatever spell had been cast on us. "It's getting late."

"Yes." I stood up and reached out a hand to help her up. "I'll see you tomorrow."

"Yes. Definitely. Tomorrow. See you." She hurried off into the darkness of the park toward her car.

I let out a disappointed sigh. It was probably better that I didn't kiss her. Kissing her would have just complicated things. I'm only in town for a few days, after all. And if I kissed her, I might not want to leave.

DECEMBER 24—THE DAY OF THE FESTIVAL

CHARLOTTE

THIS WAS IT. Showtime.

The gazebo was bathed in the colors of mismatched lights that twinkled against the darkening sky. The band had just finished sound check, and everything sounded great. The caterers had their spot to hand out free cookies and hot chocolate. Even the vendors set up without any problems.

Except for one. Mrs. Cruikshank was the owner of The Crooked Book and complained about being too close to the stage. "I'm an old woman, Charlotte. I can't be around all this noise." That was an easy fix. I helped her move her table and merchandise to a location more palatable for her.

And now, it was happening. I just had to give the Santa costume to Ivy's uncle and then I could breathe.

As the band began to play "Jingle Bell Rock" and the townspeople made their way to the park, I let myself have a minute of solace and went to the catering table. I picked up a cup of hot chocolate, reveling in the warmth and sweetness as it hit my tongue. I was exhausted from the last two days of planning and sleepless nights. Mostly because I was worried about the party. But also because I couldn't stop thinking about Sam.

I couldn't deny that there was something between us. A part of me wanted so badly to act on it. But I couldn't. The snowball fight was a great distraction from the worrying, but that was all it could be—a distraction. Even though I wanted very much to know what his full lips tasted like, I couldn't let myself go there. He was leaving in a few days, and I couldn't go through another heartbreak.

But just because I couldn't let myself go there didn't mean that I couldn't show him my appreciation for what he'd done.

I saw Sam making his way to the park along with everyone else. Nick and Rex were beside him. They talked casually as they made their way to the catering table.

"Hey, Rex," I said as I bent over to pet the dog. "Merry Christmas." The dog moved to lick me in the face, but I dodged away just in time. "And Merry Christmas to you two." The words were directed at both of them, but I only had eyes for Sam. I quickly glanced at Nick to make sure he knew I meant him too, but he was already walking away.

"Looks like the party is a hit," Sam said. "The band sounds great."

"Yeah. Everything worked out." There was a small pause, a moment of sheer awkwardness, and I knew that he was thinking about last night. I reached into my coat pocket and pulled out the gift I had made for him last night. "This is for you. To say thank you."

"No way!" Sam took the tiny paper ornament with the picture of a German shepherd inside and kneeled beside Rex. "Look, buddy. That's you. This is great. Thank you."

"No. Thank *you*," I said and felt my face burn. "That's what the ornament is for." I cringed at my own words. "Well... enjoy the festival. We have cookies." I handed him a chocolate chip cookie and regretted it. What if he didn't like cookies? I didn't want him to remember me as the woman who gave him something he didn't like. This might even be the last time I see him. The thought hit me in the chest, and I felt myself deflate.

He took a bite of the cookie and smiled. Whether it was to humor me or if he genuinely liked it, I wasn't sure. I didn't know him well enough to be able to tell. And I probably never would.

"Charlotte!" Ivy's voice pierced through the cheering crowd as the band finished their song. "Charlotte!" I saw her dodging people as she hurried toward the catering table.

"Ivy, what's wrong?"

"We have a problem. Santa's not coming."

"What?" a little boy beside Ivy asked with horror on his face. He'd overheard and immediately burst into tears.

"Oh no, it's okay, sweetie. Santa is just…" Ivy looked at me and whispered, "Santa is sick."

"Not him, too. What are we going to do?" My insides burned with anxiety. There was no way I could wrangle anyone into playing Santa now. It was too late.

Sam came over to us and kneeled beside the little boy. "Hey, buddy, don't cry. I just spoke to Santa on the phone, and he said that he can make it after all."

"Really?" The little boy perked up.

"Really. He'll be here. I promise." He stood and handed Rex's leash to me. "I assume you have the suit."

"I do. But who's going to—" He raised his brows at me and smiled. "Are you serious?"

"Yup. Give me the suit."

I jumped up at him and hugged him tightly. I couldn't help myself. Realizing what I'd done, I backed away. I felt that pull from last night, and I was glad that a crowd of people were around us.

"I'll get you the suit," I said and hurried to my car before I did something really stupid. Like actually kiss him in front of the whole town.

SAM

The things I do to prove Nick wrong.

I donned the red suit. I put on the itchy white beard that tickled my nose. Ivy even gave me a pillow to tie around my waist to fill me out.

"My uncle is pretty thin," Ivy explained when I gave her a look. "And so are you. Put it on."

I tied the thing around my waist and pulled the Santa jacket over my now misshapen belly. I probably looked silly, but I didn't care.

"Thanks again for doing this," Charlotte said when I was ready. "It means a lot."

"Of course." I almost added "anything for you" but caught myself. That's not something appropriate to say to someone who pushed you away from a kiss. I tried not to think about last night. After all, I was only a stranger who waltzed into town and would be waltzing out after Christmas. And it had to be right after Christmas, I decided. Staying any longer would just make it harder to leave.

As I made my way toward the gazebo, kids began cheering and the band played "Here Comes Santa Claus." I had to admit, I was loving the whole thing. I loved seeing the smile on the kids' faces. I loved hearing the laughter of the adults as I let out my version of ho, ho, ho because I didn't have a deep enough voice to pull it off. My brother pointed —*pointed*—and laughed, but I didn't care. I was having fun and that's what really mattered to me.

But as the festival crowd thinned and the band played their last song, something inside of me sank.

"You are a life saver," Charlotte said when I handed her the Santa suit. "You saved the festival."

"So, I'm not such a bad guy after all?"

She let out a sigh, but her smile told me she was joking. "No. You're not a bad guy at all. Maybe… if you don't have any plans for New Year's—"

"Actually, I'm leaving the day after tomorrow," I said. I hated to interrupt her, but she was about to give me an invitation that I wouldn't want to refuse. Because if she finished that sentence and we spent New Year's together, I would kiss her, and leaving would be even harder.

"Oh. Okay. Well..." She extended her hand at me, and I shook it. "It was nice meeting you, Sam DeLuca."

"You too, Charlotte..."

"Homes."

"It was nice meeting you, Charlotte Homes."

CHRISTMAS DAY

SAM

"Rex, down!" I laughed as the dog jumped up on me, begging for his new squeaky toy that I'd gotten him for Christmas. He sat down and I threw the thing into the hallway.

"Not in the house!" Nick yelled from the kitchen.

He was busy making Christmas dinner, which was just tortellini with our grandmother's secret sauce recipe. Growing up, we used to have a big traditional Italian feast, but since it was just the two of us this year, Nick made the only Italian thing he knew. I helped by procuring salami and cutting it up. I also ate most of it as we spent the morning video calling my parents, aunts, uncles, and cousins. I missed my family, but it was nice to be alone with Nick in Aurora Heights.

Still, I couldn't stop thinking about Charlotte Homes.

I went into the living room and sat on the couch, staring at the one ornament on Nick's bare tree, the ornament she had made. It was a paper cut-out of a German shepherd with the words Merry Barkmas underneath. I should've found something to give to her, something small to remember me by. I thought that I was going to forget all about her, but the more I tried to not think about her, the harder it was to stop.

"Pasta's ready!" Nick called. I watched him bring two plates of pasta to the kitchen table.

"I'll just take mine here," I said. I didn't want to leave the ornament's side.

"You will take yours at the table," he said. More like scolded. "You're not an animal."

Sighing, I got up and went over to the table to eat. My brother might be an uptight cop, but he was a really good cook. "It's good but not quite like Grandma's."

"It's never going to be like Grandma's," he said with a shrug.

I was impressed. Years ago, a comment like that would've sent him on the defensive about how spices in Italy were different and how difficult it was to make homemade pasta and the elevation wasn't right so the dough would be different anyway. He did none of that now. Aurora Heights was really good for him.

I swallowed my pasta along with the brick in my throat. I was leaving tomorrow. I was used to leaving places. I liked wandering around from place to place, finding new adventures. But for the first time in my life, I wasn't looking forward to whatever lay ahead.

"The Holiday Festival was pretty fun," he said. Finally, something to fill the silence. But thoughts of the festival just brought back thoughts of Charlotte. "You made a pretty good Santa." He stopped eating for a moment and looked me straight in the eyes. "I'm proud of you."

Warmth filled my chest. It felt good to hear those words, even if I never thought I wanted to hear them in the first place. "Thanks."

"I knew you weren't a deadbeat." He went on, but I really wished he wouldn't. "You just needed the right motivation."

"Yes, proving you wrong about me being a deadbeat was the perfect motivation." I gave him a smile.

"I don't think I was your motivation."

"What?" Heat filled my cheeks.

"You and Charlotte were getting along really nicely."

"We were. But it doesn't matter. I'm going back home tomorrow morning." I stuffed more pasta into my mouth so that I didn't have to talk about leaving and never seeing Charlotte again.

"You mean Mom and Dad's home." Nick shot me a smirk. "You know, you don't have to leave so quickly. You're welcome to stay in Aurora Heights. Try small town living for a bit. You might like it."

I already liked it. I liked the scenery and the people. I liked doing something that made people happy. Maybe Nick was right. Maybe it was time that I stopped wandering and settled down. It was time that I picked something and stuck to it. But was Aurora Heights really the right place?

DECEMBER 26

CHARLOTTE

THE PARK WAS BLANKETED in pure white from the snowfall last night. It was early morning, but Aurora Heights was already alive with people shopping, or just taking an early morning walk through the park. Snow crunched under my boots as I made my way to the gazebo.

The tables, the sound system, the Santa suit, and everything else had all been returned to the rental company. All I had left to do was to collect the decorations that Sam had brought. I assumed they were his brother's, so I would have to stop at Nick's place and drop them off.

As I unwound the lights from the rails of the gazebo I wondered if Sam had left town already. If I went to Nick's apartment, would I have to see him packing up his things? Maybe I should drop the decorations off at the police station just in case Nick was working and Sam had already left. A pang of regret hit my chest. I should've at least given Sam my number. Maybe I could find him on Facebook or something.

"Need help?" My heart skipped at the familiar voice.

"You're still here," I said. I couldn't help the huge smile spreading across my face.

"I'm still here." Sam came up the steps of the gazebo and began unraveling the lights.

"So, I guess you're leaving later today, then."

"Actually…" He stopped unraveling and came over to me. My heart hammered and I stopped what I was doing. "My brother and I had a talk and I realized something." His eyes drifted across the park for a moment. When he looked at me again, his dark eyes were filled with emotion that made my heart skip even more. "I like parties. I like having fun. I like traveling and doing things I've never done before. And there's still so much out there to do. But I want to do the one thing I've never done before."

"And what's that?" My cheeks heated from within as his gaze became intense.

"I'm going to stay. I'll be in Aurora Heights a little longer."

"Really?" A flush of tingles ran through me. I realized that we'd moved closer. We were drifting toward each other and this time, I wasn't going to pull away.

"Yes. I've had so much fun here, but I know there's more to this place. And more to you. I really like you, Charlotte." His warm hands found my cheek. "You make me want to stay."

I wrapped my arms around his neck and pulled him closer to me. "Then you better stay."

His soft lips found mine and I finally got to taste his lips. He tasted oh so sweet.

NEW YEAR'S EVE

SAM

"Nick, wake up. It's almost time." My brother was slumped in a booth at the Cozy Cat Café. He shook himself awake, then looked around with sleepy eyes.

"Where am I?" he asked.

"You're at the Cozy Cat, remember?" I said with a laugh.

In the last few days, I'd made friends with the owner, Dylan, and he invited us to a private party in the café. It was a small gathering of his closest friends. I had brought Charlotte as my date, of course, and dragged Nick out even though I knew he would just fall asleep in a corner somewhere. It was an intimate gathering, but it was the best party I'd been to in a while. And I'd been to many in my life.

"Ten seconds!" Dylan cheered as we gathered in the center of the café and counted down to a new year.

I counted down to a new me. I'd been spending almost every day with Charlotte, and I couldn't get enough. I wanted to know every little thing about her and would spend the rest of my life getting to know every detail if I had to.

Once we'd cheered and sang and toasted, I held out my

hand to quiet everyone down. "I have an announcement to make," I declared.

"Oh no, what now?" Nick groaned.

"You are all looking at the Cozy Cat Café's newest barista." I couldn't hide the pride from my voice. Everyone applauded and I bowed.

"You got a job?!" Nick and Charlotte asked simultaneously.

I put my arm around Charlotte and pulled her closer to me. I never wanted her to be away from me. "If I'm going to stay here, I'm going to need a way to make money."

"So we don't have to do the long distance thing? You're really staying?" Charlotte's smile melted my insides. There was no way I would ever get sick of that smile.

"Yup."

"Why the change of heart?" Nick asked.

I looked around the place, taking in the surroundings. I'd never felt so grounded, so rooted in one place as I had in Aurora Heights. I looked at Charlotte and said, "This place just feels like home."

THE END

ABOUT THE AUTHORS

JENNY MARIE TAYLOR is a very busy part time writer currently living in Delaware (also known as Dela-where?). She sports a master's degree in nursing education and is a full-time nursing instructor at the local community college. When she isn't doing that, she's working part time at the local hospital as a nursing supervisor. When she isn't doing that, she's yelling encouraging words at the sidelines of her kid's soccer games. When she isn't doing that, she's leading the young adult's group at church. When she isn't doing that, she's being the best wife, daughter, friend, cat and dog mom that she can be. Sprinkle in a little CrossFit, and whatever time is left to squeeze in some writing, and voila! There she is.

Visit Jenny at:
    Facebook.com/JennyTaylorsAuthorPage

PATRICIA WILSON has enjoyed a long career as a Hunter/Jumper trainer, and equestrian judge. Her life has been a true adventure, traveling the country showing horses, coaching riders, and judging competitions. Now semi-retired, she has found the time to settle down and pursue her passion for writing.

She has just finished her first novel, a historical romance, which is currently in submission. Her second novel is also a romance, set in England's Regency period. In addition to writing fiction, Patricia is a poet, claiming awards in several competitions, and a painter who sells watercolors and acrylic works regularly.

Currently, she resides in Edmond, Oklahoma with her husband and three lively terriers. Patricia enjoys writing every day, with the assistance of her favorite classical music and some strong, sweet iced tea. Her rescue mix, Finn, is always close at hand.

With degrees in education and psychology, **ANNE LUCY-SHANLEY** is a novelist based in the American Midwest. An enthusiast of all things romance, she also dabbles in dystopian, young adult, and non-fiction writing. As a firm believer in happily-ever-afters, contemporary romance remains her favorite genre.

Some of Anne's pastimes include drinking whiskey, snickering at dirty jokes, and coming up with captivating storylines while soaking in the tub. When not embracing the quiet life with a book and a cat on her lap, she occasionally travels with her husband of twenty years.

Anne loves connecting with her readers. Come join the fun at her Facebook reader group, the Saucy Society.

Visit Anne at:
   https://www.annelucyshanley.com
   Facebook.com/anne/lucyshanleywrites
   Instagram.com/writer_annelucyshanley

AMBER TERRELL grew up in the heartland of the US, the daughter of two teachers. She spent many a summer roaming darkened school hallways and pilfering abandoned libraries.

Graduating from college with a degree in psychology in 2003, she found herself drawn to the one career she said she never wanted.

Now an educator herself, she prefers to curl up with her laptop and three dogs in the evenings. When she's not writing, grading, or editing, she enjoys spending time with her daughter and husband walking the dogs, playing card games, or watching college football.

AMANDA JEMMETT began writing at a young age. She is often found with her nose in a book or her head in the clouds. After taking courses in journalism she came to the realization that writing about soulmates is her passion.

In her spare time, Amanda can be found on the ice with her son, binge-watching the next series from her thoroughly cultivated list, or singing along to an expansive array of music. She leads a simple and wonderful life in Ontario, Canada.

Visit Amanda at:
    Facebook.com/authoramandajemmett
    Instagram.com/authoramandajemmett

NIKOLETT STRACHAN accidentally discovered cozy mysteries while writing a sweet romance that was going nowhere. Deciding that her minor character, Lainey Boggins, was more interesting, she switched to writing mysteries and has never looked back. When she's not writing stories, you can find her hiking in the Canadian Rockies. She's happiest when she's curling up with a blanket, a cup of coffee, and a good book.

Visit Nikolett at:
https://www.nikolettstrachan.com
Facebook.com/nikolett.strachan
Instagram.com/nikolett.strachan

Made in the USA
Middletown, DE
04 November 2021

51695300R00106